# RETURNING

The Journey of
Alexander Sinclair

Sharon Gunason Pottinger

First paperback edition 2016

Original cover design by Trish Logan, Beyond Words, Inc. Indianapolis, IN

Author photo by Ali Cameron

ISBN 978-1-5272-0427-0

*Who are we in this complicated world?*

Rumi, 13<sup>th</sup> century Iranian poet

# ACKNOWLEDGEMENTS

I am grateful to all my friends and family who listened to the characters as they evolved and read drafts and commented. All your comments were invaluable.

Thanks to Meg MacLeod for allowing me to use a fragment of her poem, 'Sand'.

Special thanks to Kate Kasserman for her insights into the heart of the story and editorial suggestions.

Thanks also to Trish Logan (Beyond Words) for her original cover design and story suggestions.

And thanks to Sara-Jayne Donaldson (Northern Editorial) for internal design and layout.

# PROLOGUE

Alex Sinclair and his friend and colleague William Tall-grass Macdonald were riding into trouble. They'd been doing that individually and together for more than a dozen years. Alex had often worked with William. 'A seasoned veteran' Alex would call him. His editor would no doubt take out 'seasoned', but there were a lot of veterans here—most of whom had just been lucky. To be seasoned you had to have had more than luck. William had a sixth sense for the right story, the right photograph, the right moment to leave a bar.

William carefully covered his camera to protect the lens from the chronic dust of the dry, dun-coloured hills outside Kandahar. He had to be close to the action to get the kind of photos that brought the pain and the heat into living rooms and coffee shops around the world. William, after more war zones than he could name, still believed that he could make a difference with his photos.

Some people thought Alex and William got on well because they were both Scottish, but they came from different parts of that small country. Alex's Caithness accent was often mistaken for Irish; William was proud that he came from Edinburgh, the cultural and intellectual capital of Scotland. He called Alex's home the wind-blasted nose of the frozen north.

As their car was bumping along the outline of a road vaguely set apart from the surrounding landscape, William told Alex he'd been thinking of going home. Maybe taking Ahmad with him and settling down, but he didn't know where. 'I don't think my parents would know what to do with Ahmad.'

'Does Ahmad *want* to leave?' Alex asked, sidestepping the larger question of going home, something that he kept pushed well out of his own thoughts. Not many of those 'chasing the bam bam,' as their front line reporting was called, went home. Although Alex wouldn't say so, he thought William the least likely of any of them to go home. William had a vocation for his front line photography. Alex liked working with William for the energy it gave him; in return, he liked to think he gave William some much needed grounding from time to time.

'Who'd want to stay here, Alex?' William said.

'Well, we're here, aren't we?' Alex said, 'and it's Ahmad's home. It's one thing for you to play footie at Bastion with him and the others and another to take him back to Edinburgh.'

'Not Edinburgh. Canada.'

'So, a place you visited rather than a place you lived?'

'I *visited* there every summer, all summer. My grandfather –'

Their driver indicated they were nearing their destination, so Alex and William got ready. Alex slipped on sunglasses, a helmet and body armour and checked his recording device and notebooks and pencils. He liked the old fashioned tools of his trade. William had suggested Alex might get clay tablets and after filing his story, let them bake in the sun and use the clay for body armour. William pulled up his bandanna to cover his mouth and nose with one hand; his favourite camera in the other. Other equipment dangled around his neck, and the vest of many pockets held other lenses and paraphernalia within reach. 'The game's afoot,' he said to Alex and smiled, all thoughts of home disappearing. Although there was nothing to be seen through the dust and heat haze, William leaned out the window, camera in hand. Alex thought he was willing the perfect shot into being. If anyone could do it, it would be William. From somewhere a swirl of dust swallowed them all. Alex tumbled directionless, blind, choking and then there was silence and blackness.

Alex regained consciousness flat on his back in the sun-baked dust; his mouth was full of blood. He squinted into the bright sunlight scanning the colourless landscape, executing a practiced drill of assessing damage and threat. He could see their overturned car, one wheel still spinning as if expecting the others to join in, sheltering the driver, conscious but hurt. There seemed to be no immediate threat from snipers, but Alex knew they were a long way from safety. Hundreds of thousands of glass fragments lay all around them like blind eyes staring skyward.

Alex rolled unsteadily onto his side, the pain in his head making any movement agonizing. William's favourite camera was lying within his reach. Alex picked it up and began carefully brushing away the dust. He struggled then to sit up and saw the crater that the explosion had left. Their car must have tripped a tiny wire in an ugly amateurish package of anonymous destruction that had become the hallmark of this war. The driver must have managed to swerve away from the worst of the blast or perhaps the force of the explosion itself pushed them out of the kill zone.

The effort of moving forced Alex to cough violently. Some of the blood in his mouth landed near a boot. Not his boot. His mind struggled to make sense of what his eyes revealed—a boot and part of a leg. Alex realised William had gone home in perhaps the only way possible for any of them. Protectively cradling William's camera, Alex began crawling slowly toward the shelter of the ruined car.

# GOING HOME

After three days in the hospital at Bastion, Alex was declared able to travel. His concussion might still give him headaches for some time and he needed to take it easy, but he was lucky. 'If not for your helmet and the body armour…' They stopped short of saying it, but the sense was plain. If not for that—and the prompt evac—he, too, would be going home in a box. His hearing was coming back and there seemed to be no long term effects from the dust in his lungs or the fierce sun. He was lucky, he tried to tell himself as he sat in the cold military jet feeling more than hearing the drone of the engines. William was in a box at his feet. Alex was taking William's remains home. Home for William was still his parents' home. Alex's deafness had protected him from making the phone call to William's parents. The liaison officer took the number Alex offered. She also arranged space for William and Alex in the military jet whose duties include the repatriation of civilians as space is available. The British had learned over the years of empire and foreign wars to do such things with more grace than Alex would have imagined, even finding a piper in the middle of the night to see off whatever they had put into William's coffin. The sad hard truth, which he could not explain to anyone who had not been in this part of the world where death—not just death—but obliteration—is always close at hand, was that the camera bag he held on his lap held more of William's spirit than anything in that box. Alex would have to say something to William's parents and at the service, but along with his hearing Alex had lost his words: deaf and mute and alone, he didn't feel lucky.

William had spoken little of his family in Edinburgh. He had said, 'I don't think they'd know what to do with Ahmad.' William's idea about making a home for Ahmad—was it the whim of a moment? A pang of nostalgia for his own childhood? The craving for tranquillity after years of chaos could lead to nostalgic or magical thinking. Alex set those thoughts aside. First, he had to get William home.

Mr. and Mrs. MacDonald were waiting as the plane touched down. They stood erect and dressed sombrely but well. Alex became acutely aware of his rumpled, well-worn working clothes. He should have thought of that somehow somewhere in all this.

'Mr. Sinclair?

Alex nodded. 'Alex, please.'

'I'm William's father, Andrew, and this is my wife, Phyllida.'

'William's step mother,' she said without prompting, extending her hand.

'We would be honoured if you would stay at our house and attend the service for William with us,' Andrew said.

Alex hadn't anticipated this.

'Please,' said William's step mother, 'it would mean a great deal to us. To me.'

Alex nodded, not able to read the situation. As a reporter, he used to be able to size up a situation in an instant. Grief, fatigue, or perhaps he had lost whatever art had been given to him.

William's coffin was removed as decorously as it had been put on the plane. Again, there was a piper. Alex fell into step behind William's coffin. At first, slinging the camera bag over his shoulder as in the familiar pattern and then, remembering, slipped it off and held it close to him. The coffin was loaded into the hearse; Alex and William's parents climbed into another car. William now belonged to a parallel existence, separate from the living. While Alex was going to William's home; William was going into the care of those who managed the dead. Alex watched the hearse moving down the road and then closed his eyes as the MacDonalds' car started gently into motion. He was getting sentimental. He needed sleep.

The MacDonalds' house was gracious and well-appointed, a phrase from the magazines his mother liked to read in the hair dresser's, but Alex could find little of William in it. He didn't have time to look. Someone took his case and showed him to a room, where he showered, and fell into a dreamless sleep.

He woke to find clean clothes laid out for him. He was both relieved and discomfited by the gesture. When he came down for breakfast, Mrs. MacDonald offered to have his clothes washed for him. When he politely declined, she smiled and dropped her head, 'that was what William always said, too, but I knew at least that much about his life—washing machines were not easy to find.'

Alex relented. 'It has been a long time since my clothes have seen a washing machine. I'd be grateful.'

As silently and efficiently as the clean clothes had appeared, someone was dispatched to see to his laundry. Would it have been a relief or a torment for William to come back home here and try to explain or justify his ragged existence? One night in William's home was not enough to begin to answer those questions, and with that realisation came the weight of his loss. Now the infinitely many things he might have asked, might have known about his friend were irretrievably gone.

'I hope you'll come another time on a less solemn occasion. We'd like to get to know you,' William's father came into the room with the habit of someone used to walking into rooms and being in charge.

'We have your book,' Mrs. MacDonald added.

Any reply other than a grateful smile was unnecessary as the three of them stepped outside where the car was waiting.

'Today's service will be a simple interment,' Andrew MacDonald said. 'A former professor of William's now with a gallery near the art school will do a retrospective of William's work next year. I'll send you an invitation.'

'And I do hope you'll be able to come back for that?' Mrs. MacDonald picked up the thread laid down by her husband.

Were they used to working in tandem like this? Is

that what marriage is meant to be like? Through all these questions his mind kept turning over the unanswerable question—how did William fit into all this?

As the car crunched along the gravel driveway, they were silent until Mrs. MacDonald said, 'If someone says he died doing what he loved, I don't think I'll be able to bear it, Andrew.'

'Phyllida,' her husband put his arm protectively around her shoulders and eyed Alex warily, 'Remember we can't control what others say.'

'I've always hated that phrase, Mrs. MacDonald,' Alex said, uneasily navigating the sudden intimacy that William's death had thrown them into.

Only a handful of mourners attended the graveside service. Some presented letters of remembrance from colleagues around the world. Alex spoke a few—a very few words. What was it Heather had said all those years ago, 'A man of few words when it really matters.' Speaking and writing are so very different.

William's father slipped briefly out of the decorousness covering his grief in a moment alone with Alex. 'I wish I'd had a little more time with him. Losing him so completely.'

Alex hesitated. 'There's this boy,' William's father looked at him so hopefully that he felt obliged to continue. 'Ahmad was about nine when we first met him but small for his age. Almost all the kids were smaller than…'

'Yes,' Mr. MacDonald closed his eyes to shut out the hunger and hardship that William had tried so hard to capture, 'William's photographs...'

'Ahmad was one of the boys to play football with William whenever we had some time in Camp Bastion.'

'William was a joy to watch on the pitch. Such grace and speed. He left the others behind with ease,' his father said, then fell silent. Lost in grief or back on the side of the pitch watching William. Finally, he said, 'I would like you to find this boy. I want to give him a home.'

Alex had meant to offer the story as an anecdote, another memory of William to help ease his father's grief, but it felt as if it had grown into something else.

'If it makes more sense for the boy to stay there, then I am content. I just want a home for him. Our last link with William.'

'I don't know if I could find him. And finding him might well put him in more danger and destroy the home he has,' Alex said, knowing how impossible it was to explain the irrational violence to anyone who had not been there. He didn't say that he didn't think it was what William would have wanted although he was convinced of that now.

'I may be able to help. William never wanted my help, but for this boy's sake I'm sure he'd permit me to intervene.' Before either of them could say more, Mrs. MacDonald was making her way towards them, the gracious smile fraying at the edges. 'Don't say anything to my wife just yet. Until we know a bit more. I wouldn't want her to worry.'

The three of them walked to the waiting car in silence. As they arrived at the MacDonalds' home, Mrs. MacDonald said evenly but not convincingly, 'You're welcome to stay with us as long as you like.'

'Thank you, but,' Alex began and then stopped. He had

brought William home. He hadn't thought what he was doing next.

Mr. MacDonald took his cue and filled in for Alex, 'He has something he's working on,' and he looked earnestly at Alex. 'While you go on up to rest, dear, Alex and I will have a word in the study.'

Mrs. MacDonald nodded and began climbing slowly upstairs, then turned, 'If you have a home and someone there who still loves you, Alex, take the time now to make things right.'

Alex felt the full force of her loss and his own. All his thoughts about home and people he had left behind that he had kept so carefully at bay threatened now to drown him. While he spoke briefly with Mr. MacDonald, who offered to write letters and call people, which, with at least 23 separate organisations involved in the conflict in Afghanistan, was likely to be ineffective, Alex felt the pull for his own home tugging at him. It had been so long since he had been in this country. Was there anything left here for him?

Alex was candid with Mr. MacDonald. They had to remember that their presence, no matter what their intentions, might cause Ahmad more harm than good. The situation in Afghanistan was becoming increasingly chaotic and desperate. Since no one could even say if Ahmad wanted to be found, Alex thought that Mr. MacDonald would, in time, let go of his desperate, irrational hopes pinned on an unknown boy that William had befriended.

The MacDonalds' last gesture of helpfulness was to have their driver take Alex to Waverley station. He looked up at the overhead display of trains arriving, departing. He needed to go home, but where was home for him now? He'd been born in Thurso. His parents were 'atomics' because they came to Caithness to work on the nuclear power station at Dounreay. Despite having been born there, he was also an atomic. People joked that it took three generations before you were local. Lots of atomics retired in Caithness, but his parents had moved back to Yorkshire. It was home to them. It held their childhood memories and was where they courted and first set up house, but that was their history, not his. He scanned the shifting orange letters on the overhead display for the train north. Alex was relieved that the train to Inverness was on the same schedule it had been for years. If this hadn't changed, perhaps other things remained.

The train's path through the back yards and remnant places of Edinburgh contrasted sharply with the MacDonalds' lifestyle and that of the life he'd been living for so long. Too long? It was time to find out if he still had a home to go back to, or the possibility of making one.

He changed trains at Inverness for the train north, also still on the same schedule as he recalled. He had spoken with enough expats and career nomads to recognize the expat nostalgia syndrome: thinking as if once they slipped out of their home, it stayed in a suspended animation waiting for their return. He knew better, but he had nothing with which to supplant the old images. Without his journalistic mindset to hide behind, he was slipping into magical thinking, but he had a long train ride to get himself sorted. He dozed and looked out the window as the train slipped away from towns into farmland and then into open moorlands.

When he woke he noticed a piper had sat down beside

him. 'I always think this stretch of the journey is best described as a whole lot of nothing,' the piper beside him said.

'I used to think that. I've been away for a while,' Alex said.

'Wedding or funeral, loon?'

'What?'

'The kilt and coming back home: only two things bring the young'uns who've left back.'

'I've been to a funeral, but,' he shrugged, and left the sentence hanging.

'Here's a bit of white heather for luck,' the man said taking the heather from his own lapel. 'I wish better luck for you than the wedding I almost saw. Went to Dornoch and in the shade of that beautiful stained glass window, the bride was left—alone—at the altar.'

'Oh, I'm sorry.'

'Nought to do with you, loon. Here's my stop. Safe journey.' He collected his bagpipes from the luggage rack and was off the train before the weak smile faded from Alex's face.

The train lumbered on to its next to the last stop, Thurso. Alex stood up with no clear plan as he stepped onto the platform. Soft air. He had not thought of that phrase for years now, but it flew in with his first breath. He'd been many places in the world—not always hotspots or corners of desperation—none of them had soft air. The next step reminded him why so many left: an empty spot where something had been. He stared at nearly an acre and a half with rubble and weeds now where something had been.

'Big supermarket was gonna build here—so they said,'

the man who got off the train behind Alex explained. 'No one believed it. They bought it to keep someone else from having it. And then they couldn't even take out the weeds. Bloody shame.'

'I don't remember what was here before,' Alex said, peering through the chain link fence like an amnesiac.

'Auction mart,' another passenger said as he rolled his luggage towards town.

Now that he was here, Alex was at a loss what to do. There was only one person he wanted to see. Needed to see, and hoped she would want to see him. He had to steel himself for that meeting. The Royal was probably still the cheapest of the hotels in town, so he checked in, saying he wasn't sure how long he'd be staying. The girl on the desk was fresh-faced and looked about 12. He couldn't place her accent, but it was not Caithness.

So far his luck had held, so perhaps it was Open Mike night in the Comm. He'd heard someone new had bought the Commercial Hotel, but nothing seemed to have changed. He ordered a pint and fish and chips. The barman looked familiar but Alex wasn't sure. The first group on stage played traditional music—lively, good, but not spectacular. This was followed by a young girl reciting a poem to music. Alex was beginning to recall the limits of an open mike night when he heard a young girl's voice rise above the background noise, 'I could if I wanted to,' and fade again.

When he followed the sound, he saw a cluster of young—too young—people at a table near the stage. Oh Jesus, that was a chapter in his own past, sneaking in here to listen to the music with Heather. He sighed and took another sip.

He had left Heather behind. He hadn't had the courage to tell her. And now what on earth could he say to her? But he owed her something. And their daughter. He told himself he hadn't really abandoned them. He had acknowledged the bairn and he wrote and sent money and things sometimes. He turned back to the bar and hunched over his pint. He knew what he was saying was bollocks. There was no way of dressing it up even to himself, let alone Heather. What the hell had he been thinking coming back here after so long?

And then there was that same voice he had heard a moment ago at his elbow as he sat at the bar. 'I'd like a pint.'

'I need to see some ID please,' the barman said.

As triumphant as if fake IDs had just been invented, she offered a badly doctored driving license that 'proved' she was 19. The bartender, after a cursory glance, began to pull the pint. Alex took the ID out of the girl's hand. 'That's the worst fake ID I've ever seen, and I've seen a lot of them.'

'Give it back to me,' she said angrily clutching at the ID. Only then did Alex look at her and nearly fell off the stool. She was exactly like her mother—complete to the quick temper.

'Don't make any trouble, OK, now Lexie,' the barman said to both Alex and the young woman.

'Not at all. Allow me to buy the young lady a squash or an Irn Bru?'

'No, thank you, old man, I don't accept drinks from strangers,' she flounced back to her table while Alex watched her. She rejoined the group but avoided losing face about not getting the drink with a story about him no doubt. He watched as they huddled together, listening intently, and then looked up at him. He hoisted his pint to them and grinned as the circle closed in on itself again—girls giggling, young men trying on various poses of protective bravado with their assertions of what they'd do to him if he tried anything.

The music got louder as the night got later. Long after they should have been home in bed on a school night—a funny thought from a man who had only ever been a post card parent as Heather called him, Lexie and another girl were still at their table. Alex had been watching her for hours now as if in that intense watching he might see the first day of school and first steps and baby teeth. He had traded that for the life he chose. At one time he'd been so sure that was the right thing to do. Now he'd like some of that certainty back again.

The barman had been watching Alex. At first he worried about what the upshot of the fake ID spotting might be, but he hadn't actually sold her a drink, so that couldn't be a problem. Finally, near closing time, he approached Alex, 'She's young enough to be your daughter, mate.'

'I'm not your mate, and she is my daughter.'

The barman furrowed his brow and looked harder, then exploded, 'Alex Sinclair, you bastard, why the hell didn't you say so?' 'It's James Henderson. We were in school together.'

'Yes. I thought you looked familiar, but it's been a long time,' Alex smiled at the vague recollection of his school days.

The barman, lowering his voice and indicating Lexie's table, asked, 'does she know?'

'No. Yes, sort of. I mean she knows I'm her father and

she's seen photos from time to time, but she's not seen me that she would recall, and doesn't know that I'm here.'

'Well, it's a bit late, but let me buy you a whisky to wet the baby's head.'

'Thank you,' Alex said, genuinely grateful. 'I hope I get the chance to be a father.' He knew now that he wanted that, but he had no idea how. And between wetting the baby's head in the Comm and being a real father was meeting with Heather.

# HEATHER

By now, Heather would know he was back. One night in the Comm would be enough to have the story all around Caithness. That meant that he couldn't not see her, but why was he even thinking like that, the whole point of coming was to see her, wasn't it? Should he have told Lexie who he was? No. Not there in the Comm. What would he have bellowed over the music? 'Hello, you don't remember me, but I'm your dad, the guy who sent post cards and things from places around the world while you were growing up here in Thurso alone with your mum.' Jesus. Now he wasn't sure which would be worse—facing Heather or facing Lexie. What the hell did he want to happen anyway? He lay back on his bed and looked to the ceiling for answers.

He'd known Heather since they were in nursery. His parents knew her parents. Everyone thought that they would always be together. Nearly everyone. He hadn't thought about it until it was almost too late. He could never explain to Heather the feeling of being smothered, the recurring dream of drowning. Everyone gets pre-wedding jitters they'd told him. The child makes it a bit harder, but you and Heather are meant for each other, together you'll get it sorted. The day before their wedding, he left. Carefully laying the rental kit out on his bed in his parents' house, he had bundled all that he could carry for an unknown destination in his ruck sack. He walked through the night to ensure that no one who knew him saw him and talked him back. At dawn, he caught a ride in a lorry heading south.

He thought how little consolation his note, 'I will always love you,' must have been for Heather. All their subsequent communications had been short, matter of fact, his parents and hers had insisted that he look after them both. And he had. Well, sort of. The more he thought, the more he realised how selfish he had been. And now? What could he offer Heather and Lexie?

He rang her number and was relieved when the answer phone picked up. 'Hi, it's me. Alex. I'm sure you've heard I'm back in Caithness. I'd like to see you —and the bairn. Oh I guess she's hardly that any more. Well, I'll try again later.'

He felt only marginally better. He could say now at least that he'd tried, but it was going to take more than that. He had no idea what the next step was. With his mind a jumble, he couldn't bear the confines of his hotel room, especially one catering to busloads of tourists coming to Caithness looking for Brigadoon or waiting for the ferry to Orkney. He picked up his phone and his room key and set out to walk to clear his mind.

Charity shops, an empty place where the music store used to be, the town seemed less exciting now than it had been. Up the slight rise where the tennis courts were and down past the Salvation Army to the beach. He stopped at the foot of the steps, sheltered somewhat from the wind, and breathed in the damp, salty air. Gulls swirled overhead and waves hurried toward the shore carrying the energy conceived thousands of miles from here.

His first step onto the sand startled him with its softness. His footfall sank into the still-damp sand of Thurso beach where the tide had left marks of its passing. As he watched the waves and the patterns in the sand, a stanza of Heather's poetry came back to him:

> Ridge and valley scriptures in sand
> Tell of the river
> Where ruins stand,
> Lost pawns in an old game.

He hadn't understood her poetry when they were editors of the school magazine, so why on earth should he be recalling it now? While he was trying to settle himself by watching the waves, his mobile phone jangled. He jumped, trying to reach it quickly, he dropped it on to the sand, 'Oh, damn,' he muttered, hastily brushing off the damp sand clinging wilfully to the phone, and then 'hello?'

'Well, that's a fine hello.'

Jesus she must have heard. 'No, I dropped my phone in the sand. That was nothing to do with you. I mean…'

'What do you mean?'

Back footed already, he sighed and then despite the tension said, 'I'm glad to hear from you.' The sound of her voice brought good memories back to him.

'You called. I'm just returning your call,' she said.

'Well, I'm here and I thought perhaps we could…or I should…or if it's not too much trouble perhaps we might…' he stumbled hopelessly over his words.

'Come by the house about half three. Lexie comes straight home from school now because…Well, never mind that. Be here at 3:30 and we'll take it from there.'

Only after he rang off did he realise that he didn't know where she lived now. But he was still a journalist and this was Caithness. If he stopped at the Co-op to buy flowers he'd also come out with an address. Getting the address was going to be the easy part.

He walked quickly back to his hotel and showered and changed—grateful now to Mrs. MacDonald for clean clothes—and pressed—something his clothes had rarely enjoyed. What would it be like to live a life where clean clothes were routine? He checked the address in the directory. She seemed to have moved back into the house where she had grown up. In the Co-op he met a woman who'd been a friend of his mother's, so she was quick to welcome him home and help him pick flowers—one large bouquet of mixed flowers for Heather and one for Lexie, too, she suggested. He accepted her help, but balked at the suggestion of pink sweetheart roses for Lexie. His brief meeting in the

Comm suggested that her pink years—if she had ever had them—were behind her now. The woman also confirmed Heather's address and filled in the blanks. After Heather's father had died, her mother had taken a small flat in town. Yes, her mother was still here and keeping well. Heather was senior librarian now and active in several organisations in town.

Feeling as hapless as every errant lover since before the troubadours wrote ballads, Alex strode forward armed only with flowers. Once again, he thought running at least halfway around the world seemed a better choice, but it was too late for that. He'd been around the world and wound up back in the Co-op car park.

Clutching the flowers, he rang the bell at Heather's house. He felt 16 again and half expected her mother to answer. Heather opened the door quickly, 'Come in then,' she said in a tone intentionally flat. Alex remembered that tone. A veneer over a potentially explosive rage. While it was a relief in its familiarity, it was also alarming. Wordlessly, he extended the bouquets with what he hoped was a placating, cordial smile, 'A bouquet for you, and one for Lexie, too.'

'If I'd known you were at the Co-op, I'd have suggested you bring something useful for tea.'

'I'm happy to get something for tea or take you and Lexie out—pizza? Or Chinese?'

'No need. I've made lasagne. Enough for all of us, if your pressing schedule allows you to take time out to share a meal with us.'

He wanted to say his whole life was on hold after the sudden death of his friend. He needed her to talk about old times with him so he could remember who he was. He wanted to tell her he felt like he was falling, but Heather was not going to listen to him now—perhaps never.

Lexie flew into the room. Alex had forgotten how much energy a teenager contains even when comparatively still. In an instant, she recognised him from the episode at the bar. Her eyes widened and she looked first to her mother then back to Alex. Alex gave a quick shake of his head. If Heather noticed, she didn't take it in. Alex hoped it would be enough to say to Lexie, 'I didn't tell your mother…'

'Lexie,' Heather said, in a tone that Alex couldn't read, 'this is your father.'

Lexie stared at Alex intently, curiously, as if making up her mind about something. 'You don't look much like your picture,' she said, pointing to a table by the side of the sofa. Alex followed her line of sight but didn't see a photograph.

'Mum, where's that photo you always keep there on the table?'

'I don't know what you mean. Excuse me while I check the lasagne.'

As soon as Heather went to the kitchen, Lexie asked Alex, 'Why didn't you tell her? About seeing me in the Comm?'

'Just didn't seem right somehow. Is that why you have to come right home from school?'

'That. And about a million other things. I don't do anything right these days—just ask her,' Lexie angled her head toward the kitchen as she opened the drawer to the table.

'Here it is. The photograph that always sits there on the table of the two of you.'

'Actually, this is a photo of the three of us, Lexie. This is the day we found out that you were on your way.'

'But you both look so happy.'

'We were.'

'Then how come?'

'Well, it's complicated and hard to understand,' Alex said wondering if he could understand himself why he had left.

'Not hard to understand at all,' Heather said with a dangerous tightness in her voice as she came back into the room.

Alex was at a loss how to deflect the rage he felt growing within Heather.

Her face flushed now, she exploded, 'You left us behind while you frolicked around the world with bugger all to worry about.'

Alex hadn't expected a red carpet, but he was taken aback by this raw anger. He felt small and cold. Perhaps he should fight back, but Heather had always outjousted him with her quick words. He felt protective of Lexie at the same time he felt helpless.

The flowers, his offering, still lay in a heap on the table. He must have been mistaken to think he belonged here, that he could pick up the threads left so long ago. He smiled at Lexie and Heather as if he were a door to door salesman making his leave as graciously as he could manage after having the door slammed in his face. He muttered some imitation of an ordinary conversation as he stumbled his way toward the door.

Heather stood, imprisoned in the flames of her anger. Even as he left Alex knew that she would regret her words, but so much anger pushed everything else out of reach.

As he moved slowly away from the doorstep, Lexie's anxious face peered through the door, speaking hastily, conspiratorially, 'I've read your book. Mum doesn't know that. I got it in the library. She's got a bad temper, but it doesn't last.'

And then she disappeared behind the door. She was so like her mother had been. It doubled his heart ache.

He headed to the Comm. It was early and there was no music. His friend was behind the bar again. He had a dram poured by the time Alex reached the bar. After the third, the words started coming, '*With bugger all to worry about*, she said. That takes some balls. I mean excuse the inept,' and he stumbled over the word so even he knew he was drunk, 'but I was out in the parts of the world where they fucking shoot you—and then when that wasn't hot enough, for fuck's sake, I went where they blew you up from a distance. Didn't care who you were or why you were there. And I had to make sense of it all and send it back here to be read by you lot. My friend came home in a box, and I can't even say how much of him is in that box. And I had to stand and say nice things over his grave and try to fill some of the emptiness for his parents. Too much emptiness, my friend, too much emptiness.' And then there was singing. Not on the stage but with his new found friends in the bar.

# WEDNESDAYS

The sunlight was urging him awake while his eyes remained stubbornly closed. He woke finally with a start and felt his head throb. For a moment he thought he was on the road in Afghanistan wondering how much of him was left. A hangover. It's only a hangover, he smiled with the relief, but the pain was real. His smile turned more grimace as he realised there were cuts to his lip. His fingers felt stiff and he noticed bruises and swelling on his knuckles. It looked as if he had been in a fight, but that was never something he did even in his most foolish years. 'Always better to observe one than be in one,' he and William had said many times as they had left a bar just ahead of a skirmish.

William. He remembered telling the barman about William. Although it had helped for a moment to talk about William, it had not been enough to get his thoughts and feelings to settle down into a coherent narrative. A story to be filed and sent out all carefully controlled. He was adrift with no haven in sight. A wave of nausea washed over him. He knew he would feel better after vomiting, but it meant moving and that meant pain all over. He hadn't felt this bad since the jungle-hiking days in Guatemala. Or maybe Sri Lanka? He had become an old man early, jumbling up his countries and his maladies in his mind. And for what? Before he could finish writing his epitaph, the phone rang. He winced at the pain of the sound and hastily retrieved his phone, 'Yes?' was all he could manage.

'Despite the terrible example you set for your daughter last night,' Heather's voice sounded like an actor overdoing righteous indignation, 'you can come Wednesday afternoon after school—I'll be out—you can help Lexie with her homework. She's not doing well in school—maybe you can be some help there.' And she rang off without waiting for a response.

He had forgotten how Heather used to boss him about. Well, he'd said that he wanted to be a real father and helping with homework was as good a way as any. For the moment the larger concern was figuring out how to live in a place where other people not only knew his business, but, in this case, knew more about it than he did.

By the time he had showered and emptied himself of some of the poison from the night before, he was hungry. He wanted the comfort of a teetering table in the edge of the bakery with ladies in pastel uniforms like he remembered. He wanted—more than wanted—he needed someone to be nice to him. And they were. They fussed over him as if he were the prodigal son. One of the women who came into the bakery while he was eating had even read his book. Where had he been lately? Oh. Afghanistan. Was he going to write about that, too? Well, she hoped so.

Perhaps he would find the words for Afghanistan in time, but for now he had to find his way in this world. The world of parents helping with homework. If he had hung up his freelance reporting, he had to find a way to earn a living, too. Royalties from his book had never been large and they dwindled over time as books like his grew stale. If he called his agent she would ask about his next book and he couldn't tell her that any gift for words had disappeared in the bomb blast. His hearing had returned, but that place where words had danced in his head was silent.

So what do 16 year olds these days read in English class? And why was Lexie not doing well in school? And what on earth could he do about it? He looked at his watch. If he walked quickly he might still find his old teacher, Mr. MacLeod, in his office. He'd be able to help. And it would be good to see him.

Ian MacLeod was headmaster now rather than English teacher. Mr. MacLeod—you can call me Ian, now, Alex—was genuinely happy to see him. Alex was relieved. What had he expected? His old teacher spoke freely and generously about the curriculum and expectations for students in Lexie's year, but explained that he couldn't say anything specific about Lexie without the express permission of her mother because Heather was the custodial parent. Before Alex had finished nodding, assuring his former teacher he had no intention of pressing him for details, Ian MacLeod added, 'It would be fair to say that she is her mother's daughter.'

Alex smiled. He felt certain that was meant to help him, but he didn't understand how. He shook hands with his mentor and headed out into the twilight with his information, including an address in one of the old wooden houses built for the atomics. It was used now by temporary staff and visitors as they were dismantling the plant. There was a room there that Alex could use for a while. Another young clerk was at reception as Alex checked out. He yearned for a conversation with someone that knew him or feigned interest. The clerk, perhaps because of limited language or training in a more formal culture, was matter of fact about his leaving. Alex had to be content that the move would mean a relief to his finances and he might have some company as well. His first home had been one of these wooden houses. He hoped they had weathered at least as well as he had.

Wednesday he rang the bell as nervous as any actor auditioning for a role. Lexie answered the bell and stepped aside to let him in, neither hostile nor welcoming.

'Would you like a cup of tea or something?' she asked.

'If you're having something, otherwise, no.'

'I get a snack after school. I'll put the kettle on.'

He followed her to the kitchen and saw schoolbooks stacked on the table.

She put the kettle on and began making an egg salad sandwich for herself.

'These are your school books, are they?'

'No. Modern sculpture.'

He said nothing in reply but picked up the books one by one. Some he recognized, most he didn't. He said as much.

She shrugged and began eating as if the sandwich provided a wall to hide behind.

'The only thing I recognise here is the Shakespeare. Which one are you studying?'

'Macbeth.'

'Would you mind reading a bit of it out loud to me?'

'Which part?'

'Anything you like.'

'I'll try to find something worth reading—so much of this is boring,' she said leaving behind the crusts of her sandwich and picking up the book.

He steeled himself for murder and mayhem, which she delivered with gusto and genuine feeling for the words.

'Good. That's good. You have a nice voice.'

'But?' she asked defensively.

'But what?'

'What did I do wrong?

'Nothing that I could see. I just wanted to hear you read to see if you stumbled over the words or didn't seem to understand it, but you were great, really. You read so well that I could hear the poetry in his language…'

'Did my mum tell you?'

Perhaps he should have said 'Tell me what', but he said instead, 'Your mum isn't talking to me,' which seemed to cover all possibilities.

'Then MacLeod. They're both at me about this poetry thing.'

'Well, this is the first I've heard about it, so I'm not part of the conspiracy.'

She looked up with what was maybe half a smile and confessed, 'I don't get poetry.'

'What exactly don't you get?'

'Why don't they just say what they mean?'

'Oh.'

'What does that mean? That's why you're here, right—another person mum has on her side to tell me how stupid I am.'

'That's a lot to assume from my just saying "oh". When I was your age, I didn't get poetry either.'

'And now?'

'Depends on the poem. A poem is like a code. If you have the key, then it reveals more than a straightforward prose piece.'

She sat across from him, arms folded across her chest, but she was not actively resisting, so he soldiered on. He started with poems about place and they worked their way through Norman MacCaig's, 'Below the Green Corrie.'

One Wednesday was hardly enough to make a difference in her schooling or his parenting, but he felt triumphant nonetheless. He began to measure his life in Wednesdays as the initial awkwardness dissipated and they developed a routine. Lexie usually had a question for him as soon as she opened the door. He enjoyed her questions. Was he following the curriculum or helping—he hoped so, but he loved the time with Lexie.

He was usually leaving as Heather returned from her job at the library. No one had talked about it. It just seemed easier that way. There was no obvious tension, but any words exchanged were matter of fact: a brief exchange about the topic of the day or some measure of progress or even the universal pastime of comments on the weather as he bundled up his books and papers and Heather and Lexie settled into their tea time ritual. He didn't allow himself to think that he might somehow fit into that routine. He was content to be putting one foot in front of the other in this new role of part-time parent.

Alex and Lexie were so intent on their reading, they didn't hear the door open earlier than usual. Heather stormed into the kitchen waving a folded newspaper above their heads. 'What is this, then, Alex? A publicity stunt? A little time between assignments to hob nob with the natives?'

Alex was too baffled to say anything, but Lexie said, 'What are you on about, mum?' as she stood up and took the paper from her mother's hands. Heather then turned her attention entirely toward Alex, still seated with the poetry book open in his hands, struggling to make sense of Heather's sudden attack.

'I was just doing what you asked...'

'I never asked you to come in here and make a fool of us.'

'Heather, calm down a sec and tell me what's going on.' As soon as he said it, he realised how wrong it was. 'To one who is beside himself, no prospect is so distasteful as that of self-recovery.' He kept that quote from *Death in Venice* on his laptop. He had interviewed psychotic generals and talked his way out of the gun sights of illegal loggers in rainforests by keeping that truth in mind. Why had he abandoned it now when he most needed it?

Lexie came up to her mother with the newspaper in hand. 'Is this what you're upset about?' she pointed to an article headlined, 'Celebrated Thurso Graduate Returns to Caithness.'

Alex stood to see the article and to put some distance between himself and Heather. Her anger unsettled him and made him worry about Lexie. A small piece in the local paper about him. His agent must have done that, and the local editor took it off the wire. No one had contacted him. A quick glance suggested it looked like standard verbiage. He couldn't understand why it had angered Heather. He looked up at her naively, 'My agent must have sent something out…'

'Oh, "my agent"', she mocked.

'Heather. Please. I didn't have anything to do with this. Whatever has upset you, I'm sorry.' Then, in a softer tone he added, 'I don't want Lexie to see us argue.'

'*You* don't want Lexie to see us argue. That's fine. I've raised her all on my own and now you waltz back in here "between assignments" to God knows where and try to tell me how to raise my daughter.'

'Heath, please.'

'Don't you "Heath" me, you bastard. Get out. Get out! Get out and don't ever come back again unless you come back in a box like your friend.'

Alex recoiled from her anger. Her last words had with the precision of the surgeon's scalpel removed the tentative healing of his grief and dislocation. His vision narrowed, the colours drained out of his sight. He put out his arms to feel for the doorway that he knew was close by. Stiff-legged, slowly like the wounded creature he was, he turned toward the safety of the door. If he had seen the look on Heather's face, he would have realised that even in her desperate anger she knew she had gone too far, but she could not or would not take back the wounding words. The last thing he heard as the door closed behind him was Lexie's voice, 'What about me?'

He walked. He had seen men who were wounded, sometimes near death, walking. Refusing to stop. He had seen medics walking alongside them to render what help they could. Alex had always thought they were walking home. In their mind's eye they saw some place of comfort or where they were needed. Now bitterly he thought they, like him, were just walking away.

By the time he had walked along the beach, into town and around the river and up the steps toward the cemetery, avoiding the long rows of headstones, to reach the ridge of the hill, he had calmed enough to begin taking stock. So Caithness was not going to be home. He could make some kind of a living even if it were just lectures on old adventures or picking up the threads of his first plan—to teach. He had enjoyed the time spent with Lexie.

Lexie. If not for Lexie, he could pack his bag tonight. Her plaintive voice to her mother echoed in his head, 'What about me?' He leaned against a tree and cried for all the people he loved and could not reach. Darkness fell and with it came a chilling wind that made him aware that even though he had no answers, he had to do something. He wiped the worst of the mud from his shoes and headed back toward his room in the wooden house like the one he was born in. Like it, but not the same. Nothing stayed the same.

He hunched up his shoulders to keep what little warmth he could as he walked quickly home, but the wind whipped away the warmth as soon as he created it. Within a few yards of his house, he saw an odd shape in front of the door. A parcel? A person? He was wary of odd shapes in the dark—habits of places where anything out of the expected meant trouble. But this was Caithness. He moved ahead less cautious, more curious. It looked like…He quickened his step. 'Lexie! What are you doing here?' She had folded up her legs to pull her school sweatshirt over them—even so she was shivering from the cold. He pulled off his thin jumper and wrapped it around her shoulders then pulled her gently upright, 'I know you feel stiff and don't want to move right now, but it's best—really. Can you talk?'

She shook her head No.

'Does your mother know where you are?'

This time she shook her head vigorously No and threatened to wriggle away from Alex. 'OK, OK, I'll stay with you. You're all right, but we need to tell your mum you're OK. You don't have to say it, Lexie. You think your mum doesn't care, but she does. She can be clumsy about it, but she loves you.'

Steadying Lexie against him, he reached in his pocket for his phone—damn. He had left everything still sitting on the table at Heather's. Lexie could walk. He would just walk her back home. It was slow going with Lexie, but she seemed content to be guided by him and in time he felt her small frame easing and she warmed up enough to talk.

'That article said you were hurt in Afghanistan?'

'Yes.'

'Who was it that got killed?'

'William Tallgrass MacDonald, a photographer, and a friend of mine.'

'Why did you become a journalist?'

He hadn't been prepared for this question from his daughter.He must have answered it in interviews a thousand times, but this was different. 'Because of you actually.'

'Did you hate me so much?'

'Not at all. Just the opposite—you remember that photograph you showed me?

'The one on the table with you and mum smiling?'

He nodded. 'I was at Uni studying English literature…'

'That's why you sound like a teacher?'

'I guess so. When we knew you were on the way, we needed some money quickly, so I took a Journalism course. I started writing little things then while I finished my degree. And then bigger pieces from further away.'

'Mum said you went away because of me, but I thought she drove you away—like she did tonight.'

He felt like an ice skater striding out over unknown parts of the ice and wondering if it would hold. He swerved the well-defined crack in the ice about her mother and answered in a smooth, journalistic tone, 'Well, you led me into journalism and that led me away, so you could say I went away because of you, but I think that middle bit is important.' He stopped and turned to face her, 'I loved you, Lexie, and your mum.' He could hear her thinking—or perhaps he was trying to sort his own thoughts for the inevitable questions—If you loved us, why did you leave? and why did you come back?

'Do you have your key?' he asked Lexie as they stood in front of her door.

She shook her head No.

He stepped around her to ring the bell and then stood anxious, not knowing what sort of reception to expect with his hands on Lexie's shoulders—protecting her or hiding—he couldn't say which.

The door flew open and Heather rolled Lexie into her arms, 'Oh My God, Oh My God. I thought I'd lost you. I've been so worried.'

Thus Alex became redundant. He might have turned and slipped away except for the awkwardness of the essential bits of his life left on their kitchen table.

'Come in. Come in, both of you,' Heather said, looking up at him tentatively.

Once inside he noticed his muddy shoes and stood awkwardly on the too-small door mat, pinioned between the easy intimacy of slipping his shoes off to join the others by the side of the door or lingering on the edge.

Over her shoulder as she bustled Lexie upstairs for a warming bath, 'Put the kettle on, will you? You must need a cup of tea, too.'

He slipped off his shoes and stepped into the kitchen to do as he was told. Alex was beginning to pace when Heather finally came into the kitchen with his jumper folded over her arm. She extended it to him, 'Thank you.'

It astonished him that the same person who had loomed so large only a few hours ago now seemed so small and fragile. He slipped the jumper over his head. He was still chilled.

'Lexie's OK then?' he asked.

Heather nodded. 'Warm bath and then straight to bed. I stayed with her until she was asleep.'

'Good. I'll be off then.' He picked up his phone and other bits from the table.

'I've put some blankets and a pillow on the sofa. It's so late now. Not very comfortable, but I can make you a good breakfast to make amends.'

The sofa was uncomfortable, but he'd slept on worse. He woke to the smell of coffee—good coffee—and bacon freshly grilling. He folded up the covers and returned the small Afghan carpet to centre stage on the back of the sofa.

On one of her trips moving into and out of the scene like a frenetic bit player in a farce of domestic life, Lexie stopped long enough to look at the carpet and tell him, 'I used to pretend that was a magic flying carpet that would take me to faraway places.'

'It's from Afghanistan. That friend of mine I told you about…'

'William?'

'Yes, he knew a lot about carpets. An Afghan friend of ours had a store and they made their carpets. It was wonderful to watch them. Each of these knots is hand tied.'

Alex thought the conversation was probably lost in the morning mayhem of Lexie looking for this and then that and lamenting the various elements of the day in front of her. He marvelled at the grace with which Heather parried each whinge or question. If Lexie felt any of the effects of the emotional storm of the night before, she gave no sign of it, disappearing hurriedly, cheerfully, out of the house in a cloud of energy.

The silence after the door closed behind her was a relief; Heather sighed and sank into a chair at the kitchen table with cup in hand. After a moment, she looked at his plate, 'Want some more?'

'No thanks. It was wonderful. But that's plenty. Thank you.' Without Lexie as an excuse or a buffer between them, Alex sat cautiously wondering what might be coming next.

'I'm the one who should thank you,' Heather spoke without a trace of the anger or indignation he'd been facing for so many weeks now.

He waited, anxious, wondering where the conversation was going.

'For bringing Lexie home for starters,' she continued, as if in response to an unspoken question. 'It would have been easy to tell her how horrid I was and do I don't know what…'

'I would never do something like that,' he hoped he kept the hurt and the anger out of his own voice. He had done a bad thing leaving her, leaving them, but he was not such a bastard. In his own mind, he had been faithful to Heather, but he realised how little he had offered for Heather to believe in him.

'I know. I know. But…'

Alex folded his hands and waited. Hard words flew out of Heather's mouth, but the softer ones took longer.

'It hasn't been easy,' she said. 'That's not a criticism of you,' she added. 'It seems like ever since you came back I've done nothing but get at you.'

He didn't need to say that he understood her anger or appreciated how difficult it must have been. It would be patronising at best and possibly derail wherever their first genuine conversation might be going, so he kept still.

'But when I read in that newspaper article what they

said about being 'between assignments' I felt again all the anger of that first leaving. It was as if it were happening all over again. I couldn't bear it.'

'That article,' he said, pulling the paper toward him, '*between assignments* means, basically, unemployed. And the headline, *Celebrated Thurso Graduate Returns to Caithness*—what twaddle—it could as easily have said, *shell-shocked, combat-weary hack comes back to the only place that was ever home and tries to pick up the pieces of himself.*'

Heather looked up at him, tears brimming in the edges of her eyes and reached out her hand to stroke his cheek. 'I believed you would come back. But it has been such a very long time.' He put his hand over hers and felt a completeness like the last piece of a jigsaw clicking into place.

She drew her hand away and smiled. 'I don't know where we go from here.'

It was a moment in which he might have said how much he loved her or that he was grateful to have the chance to start again or how happy he was to see that Lexie was more wonderful than he could have dreamt or any of so many things that would have been infinitely better than, 'I don't know either.'

And she might have flown into a rage and said it was his job to know those things or that was a fine way to start a relationship once again leaving all the work to her or who did he think he was waltzing back in here after all those years. Instead, she laughed even as the tears ran into the corners of her mouth and shook her head, 'Aren't we a pair of numpties?'

He didn't need to say yes.

'I'll do the washing up,' Alex said, moving toward the sink almost as if he belonged.

## DÉTENTE

Words began to come back to Alex. Lesson plans for Lexie, notes on poems read or re-read, and a journal for himself. Private words. Healing words. Writing his way back home. This writing grew into little articles for Walking magazine and other niche markets and travel 'zines as well as book reviews for a friend's web site. It paid little or nothing, but his life was like a board game where he had gone back to some step he had missed and was starting over.

Wednesdays were still just for Lexie, but Mr. MacLeod had helped him find a few more students, so he had Tuesday and Thursday sessions in the library. Heather always managed to be somewhere else in the library when he was there to avoid the smiling glances of her colleagues. Some things hadn't changed in the intervening years.

Between preparing for his tutorials, he walked and he read. He kept a reading log and notes on each of his student's progress. His freelance life had meant he was always on call. Rather than being independent as he and his colleagues thought they were, they were completely tied to outside events. His life had been subordinated to the periphery of other people's lives. He had not been the centre of his universe; he had been someone else's moon.

Alex had not been to visit his parents since his return. Something his mother regularly pointed out in his weekly phone conversations with her. Alex picked up the phone for what he thought would be a quick conversation with his mum. How's Lexie? Fine. Heather? Fine. Lexie's birthday coming up, isn't it? Yes, yes. Of course he had forgotten and she knew it. Perhaps you could bring Lexie for a visit for a birthday present to her? You still like trains, don't you? School, mum. Can't take Lexie out of school. After a suspiciously long pause, 'How are you and Heather? Don't say *fine*, Alexander.'

Something rattled through his letterbox while he searched for another noncommittal word to replace 'fine.' He thought idly how loud a single piece of junk post could be. 'Getting late, mum, gotta go. Lexie will be home from school soon and exams are coming up. We have lots of work to do.'

If she sighed, he didn't hear it as he rang off.

'Détente,' détente was the word to describe Heather and himself. An easing of tensions. A temporary cessation of hostilities that might lead to something or not. He was glad he was hundreds of miles from his mum. Just her question was enough to make him edgy. He picked up the books and papers for Lexie's session and headed for the door. In the post, rather than the usual grocery store flyer, was a proper envelope. He picked it up and scanned the carefully handwritten name and address on fine paper, then, turning it over, read the MacDonalds' Edinburgh address. They had said he would be invited to William's photographic retrospective but just handling the envelope filled him with an unease, a reminder of the life he had left behind. He threw it, unopened, among the books and papers in his hands and hurried to the safety of poetry and his new life with his daughter.

'What's this?' Lexie asked, finding the envelope among the essays from their last session that Alex had marked for her.

'A letter.'

'Why haven't you opened it?'

'I just got it.'

'Do you know who it's from?'

'William's parents.'

'Don't you want to know what it says?'

'I don't want to lose any of our time on unrelated things.'

Lexie looked at him curiously. Jesus, how like her mother she looked—that same I-know-you-are-avoiding-something expression, but she nodded and picked up her essays, 'What does this squiggly mark here mean?'

They settled into working, and the cream envelope with the blue lettering sat, almost invisible, in the middle of the table. Heather came in with takeaway Indian for them all.

'Set the table, will you, Lexie?'

Lexie nodded, carefully handing the envelope to Alex, then collecting the rest of the papers into a rough stack on a chair while she got mats and napkins and silverware.

'Nice surprise, Heather, thank you,' Alex said.

'I thought you might be getting dishpan hands from all the washing up.'

Alex looked into her smile and felt the universe open up for him, but then quickly looked down at his books.

'He got a letter today from William's parents,' Lexie said.

'How are they doing?' Heather asked Alex.

'He hasn't opened it yet,' Lexie said before Alex could respond.

'Oh,' Heather said, 'well that's not really our business, I guess.'

'Oh, no, I don't mean to be secretive. It's just that…,' Alex began.

'It makes you sad because it reminds you of your friend,' Lexie offered to finish his thought for him.

'Well, yes, Lex, that's true but…'

'I have a bottle of wine that just might take this meal from prosaic takeaway to haute cuisine,' Heather offered as a conversational bridge to somewhere, anywhere other than where Alex was floundering.

'How about some for me, too?' Lexie asked, casting a quick, testing glance at Alex.

'No,' Alex and Heather both said, and then Alex said, 'I mean, whatever your mum says.'

'I have some fruit juice or some sparkling water, a little bit festive,' Heather said trying to be conciliatory.

'Yeah, "festive", right,' Lexie sulked more for appearance than genuine discontent. Alex suspected that she liked being sheltered by the both of them. The meal felt like a celebration. The three of them lingered talking and nibbling until Lexie was reminded of her bedtime and hugged them both goodnight.

'Well, if there are no dishes, I'll be off then.'

'How about finishing the wine with me?'

Heather poured fresh glasses for them both and they sat in the sitting room. She pulled the band off her ponytail and let her hair fall loose around her shoulders, then kicked off her shoes and folded them underneath her on the sofa. Alex hadn't seen Heather so relaxed in the months now that he had been coming to the house.

'I wanted to talk to you.'

Alex held his breath. Was this the end of the détente?

'I was wondering if you'd help me figure out what to do for Lexie's birthday. You've spent a lot of time with her lately, and,' she shrugged leaving the thought like an open invitation.

'I'm not sure what I can do,' Alex said thinking both of all the birthdays he'd missed and the odd delight he felt now about being part of one.

'Well, think about it. We have some time so thought I'd mention it now. She has a couple of close friends. We might do something with them all.'

Alex nodded and sipped his wine, wondering if the close friends were the same ones he'd seen with Lexie in the Comm.

She refilled their glasses and said, 'I also realise how little I know about your life since you left.'

Alex tensed again.

'And I'd like to. God, I know it's trite as hell but we weren't just—well, you know, romantically involved. We shared interests and ideas. I miss that.'

'I've missed you, too.' It sounded lame, but he felt his chest ease as the words slipped out of him.

'I've been thinking about this for a while but seeing that envelope from William's parents, and your reluctance about it, made me realise that,' she took another gulp of wine 'that I had lost parts of myself. Do you know what I mean? Or is that just the wine talking?'

'I do understand' he said more confidently than he felt— would he ever really understand Heather?—'whether it's the wine or not,' finishing his and standing. 'Now I should be going.' For some time now he had been thinking so much about kissing her and pressing her body against his that her words had been reduced to background music. She rose, and tottering, he reached out to steady her. She smiled up at him and kissed him—gently, effortlessly, as if they had never been apart. 'I'm glad you're back, Alex. Good night. Come by tomorrow afternoon. It's half day in the library. We'll talk.'

The cold night air helped clear his head as Alex stepped across the threshold. He took the long way back to his house walking under a deep black sky with stars so sharp and clear they looked to him as if they had just been born and glowed with the joy of their own creation. Anthropomorphizing the stars, he chuckled to himself. Had he talked with Lexie about that? He fumbled in his pocket for his notebook. Lexie had a mind that could take in as big an idea as he could conjure for her and quickly make it her own. The

Tuesday-Thursday bunch, however, were not so quick or so inventive. He tried to imagine a life of students like the Tuesday-Thursday bunch stretching in front of him and sighed, shoving the notebook back in his pocket.

Back in the empty kitchen of the wooden house he called home for now, he sat down at the table and opened the envelope, the invitation to the exhibit of William's photos fell out: 'Alexander Sinclair and guests' he read and smiled, thinking 'the three of us.' The three of us, God, he liked the sound of that. Nothing could replace William, but there had been an emptiness in his life that he'd been able to ignore as long as there was William and one more story to chase.

Mrs. MacDonald had written a note with the invitation. Simple, gracious. Would he and his guests be able to join them for dinner the day before the opening? She hoped also that they would be willing to stay at their home and attend the opening with them. He liked the idea of Lexie walking down the long stairs of the MacDonalds' house running her fingers over the balustrade, no doubt struggling to resist the impulse to slide down it. And Heather? What would she make of the MacDonalds, their house, William's photos? His life away from her? He picked up his journal and wrote his fears and hopes into the plain white paper and closed the cover as if filing a story and thus letting go.

Alex took a morning run under a sky full of the clear light that characterizes spring, a season in Caithness noted more for the return of light than for its warmth. Laundry on the line waved like flags in the gardens as he ran by. He stopped by the Co-op and picked up wine and rolls and fruit and cheese and forks and plates and a cool bag to keep it all in. Then he showered, changed, and hurried to meet Heather as she was leaving the library. He thought they'd go to Duncansby Head and then down to the sheltered beach of Sannick, where it would be warm, to enjoy their lunch.

'Oh! I thought you were coming to the house' she said, perhaps slightly embarrassed as her colleagues looked at Alex and smiled.

Ignoring their looks, but noting Heather's unease, Alex held up the cool bag. 'I thought we might have a picnic. The day is so fine.'

Heather seemed to be working something over in her mind when she smiled and said, 'Yes, good idea, but I'll need to stop home and change first.'

Alex never expected to understand women and their clothing rules, so he accepted it without question and climbed into the car beside her. 'It's been a long time since I drove a car,' he said.

'How so?'

'The places I've been were not safe or cars were scarce.'

'I've read your book. I didn't tell Lexie that I had, but I did, so I know a little bit about where you've been, but it does not say much—directly, at any rate—about you.'

'It's easier to tell other people's stories—and more important—than telling my own. The hardest part of the book was my own bio.'

'Lexie has a box underneath her bed of newspaper clippings about you. She doesn't think I know about that either.'

'Och those stories are made up by someone else. Sometimes they don't even get the facts right, let alone the important things.'

'What are the important things, Alex?' Heather asked with no apparent trace of her previous indignation.

'I've come home, Heather, to find that out. If I'd stayed here, I—we—might have lost our connection anyway. You, Lexie, the three of us that's important. I know that now.'

The cool bag and the invitation lay on the kitchen table while Alex and Heather made love upstairs in the same room where they had first discovered sex in stolen moments between school and the return of her parents. At first, now, as it had been then, it was an awkward mixture of eagerness and anxiety, but then time relaxed and they eased into a graceful rediscovery of the curves and the rhythms of each other's bodies. As Heather dozed in Alex's arms he whispered, 'Patient Penelope, fighting off the eager suitors, I'm glad you waited for me.'

Heather chuckled.

'I thought you were asleep.'

'Umm hmm. Not so asleep to let you start making classical allusions without me—or about me. It's a good thing you went into journalism, you wrote rubbish poetry.'

They both laughed. Holding her close, he felt her laughter and his as one.

'Mum,' Lexie called up the stairs, 'I'm home.'

By the time they had collected themselves and come downstairs, Lexie had set the table and spread the picnic lunch out for tea. Before Heather or Alex could offer any of their considered words of explanation, Lexie grinned up at them, 'I thought you might be hungry,' and then taking them both in added, 'and since it's a celebration, I've set a wine glass for me, too.'

Together they ate the picnic lunch for dinner and talked about the invitation from the MacDonalds. Although Heather and Lexie were keen to go, they had to figure out about time away from school and new dresses and so many things. Alex drank his wine and realised how complicated life was when it included more than himself.

He kissed Heather goodbye after Lexie went to bed.

'You're not staying?'

'I need to get my things and give Lexie a little time to get used to having someone else around all the time.'

Heather nodded. If she felt any anxiety about his leaving, Alex didn't notice.

He walked slowly homeward, then amended 'home' to 'the place where he'd been staying.' Wherever he was staying no matter how long had always been called home. It seemed easier. Most of his colleagues did, too. The ones who had no real home. It took him only a few minutes to pack. He wrote briefly in his journal and then slept. After sixteen years, he was finally going home.

Heather and Alex were married quietly in the registrar's office. Lexie, having turned 16 a few days before, was a witness; Ian MacLeod, their former teacher, the other witness. Alex called his parents after the wedding, then Heather's mum set up a three-way video call so they could all see each other to celebrate. If anyone said, 'It's about time,' or sniggered and said, 'In my day, it was marriage first and then bairns,' as surely someone did, Alex didn't hear it and wouldn't have cared.

The three of them began their family life together planning their trip south for the exhibition of William's photographs. Alex pushed for the train south when he discovered that Lexie hadn't been beyond Inverness—smoothing over Heather's bristling at the suggestion that her parenting was somehow deficient—by pointing out that the train would give her the opportunity to enjoy the scenery as well.

They broke their journey in Inverness, staying the night in the Station Hotel—no one called it by its new name. Lexie climbed the broad staircase and looked at the artwork on the landing turned gallery. They lunched and took in Flora MacDonald's statue and the museum. Lexie expressed her disappointment in so much culture when there was shopping available, but it seemed more whinging for effect than disappointment. Alex was learning to read his daughter. After Lexie had gone to bed, he and Heather had a late supper and walked along the Ness. As they lingered on a pedestrian bridge overlooking the fast moving water below, Heather said in a statement-question, 'The MacDonalds are picking us up?'

'I expect they'll send their car.'

'It seems—awkward—imposing on them in their grief. They're strangers, after all. Or I should say—we're strangers to them, at least Lexie and I are.'

'I never met them before—' Alex hesitated as the image of that day came roaring into his unguarded memory, then settled himself and said simply, 'Before,' safe in the knowledge that Heather needed no further explanation. Heather moved closely up against him and he put his arm around her. 'You're cold. How about a drink in the bar? Perhaps if we tell the barman we're newlyweds, he'll treat us to a dram.'

The hotel bar was quiet on a midweek, still-early night. He and Heather enjoyed coffee with brandy. Alex ordered a dram for himself as Heather lingered over her coffee.

'Truth is. Without William I would only ever have been page 37,' Alex said.

'Page 37? 'Heather asked gently, knowing that these words hadn't come easily from Alex.

'Something Tony Lloyd said. He's been around a long time and he's both successful and recognized—most of us are lucky to have one or the other but to have both—well, he's looked up to. He was quoted as saying that if you had the choice of death, glory, or getting a story on page 37—no one ever reads that far these days—he would opt for a story on page 37. Not altogether true, of course, but it makes a good quote,' he smiled ruefully and stared into his glass.

'So William…,' Heather prompted.

'He was front page stuff. His photos—well, you'll see for yourself Friday night at the opening—his photos are stories in themselves. He didn't need me. He said he did—he probably told his parents that. I think that's why they set such store by me.'

'I've read your words, Alex. Even when I hated you, I loved your words. You have a power to tell a story that always made me jealous.'

Alex smiled up at her. Maybe with her faith he'd find those words.

Alex and Heather were settling into sleep as he felt himself drifting back to Afghanistan. He shook himself awake and wrote in his journal, then he eased back into bed and curled into the curve of Heather's sleeping back and tried to match the rhythm of her breathing with his own. He must have slept, but for how long he couldn't say. He was under fire and running down an alley that went on and on, his terror rising at each step. One by one the soldiers he was following vanished. He was alone with gunshot and whispers all around him. Suddenly, William stepped out of a doorway and beckoned him into the safety of an empty house, but in that instant of his stepping out, a sniper's bullet whistled through William's head. He fell, still smiling at Alex. Then Alex was awake with Heather leaning over him, clearly worried. The bed clothes were scattered. He was soaked with sweat. 'It should have been me,' he said. 'Not William. I was meant to look after him.'

Heather straightened the bed clothes and wiped his face and hands with a warm cloth and pulled his damp T shirt over his head replacing it with a dry one. 'You have time to sleep before we have to go. I'll stay with you. Sleep now.' She had begun to understand the price Alex had paid for his life apart and was worrying now about what else this trip would uncover for the two of them.

Alex woke to the clatter of dishes and the smell of toast. Heather had ordered room service and she and Lexie were enjoying their fry up. 'I think yours is still warm, Alex. We didn't want to wake you.'

'I've decided 'Dad' is too American, but 'Father' sounds awfully formal,' Lexie announced. 'What do you think I should call you now?'

'Let him have his coffee first, Lex. No one can think before coffee.'

Back on the train south, Lexie decided to trial both

names in an animated conversation about the things sliding by the train's window, fellow passengers, friends at school or the myriad big and little things that make up traveller's conversations. Heather read a book, joining in the conversation from time to time. Alex felt cocooned from the effects of his nightmare, safe with his family, as the train rumbled along the tracks

# WORDS AND PHOTOGRAPHS

When they arrived at Waverley station, Lexie was delighted to see a man standing with a small sign, 'Sinclair' scanning the passengers arriving. Alex was pleased to see Lexie so excited. He had missed so much of her growing up.

The driver recognised him, 'Mr. Sinclair!' Smiling at Heather and Lexie as he took their bags, 'and this must be your family. I'm glad to see you all. Mr. and Mrs. MacDonald said they would delay lunch if the young lady would like a brief tour of the city,' he looked at Heather and Alex. 'I understand this is her first visit to Auld Reekie.'

Alex stifled a laugh to see Lexie's eyes glowing with anticipation. He looked at Heather, who said to the driver, 'That would be much appreciated, thank you.'

Alex suspected that Lexie would remember more about the inside of the car than Edinburgh's historic sites, but her excitement electrified the atmosphere in the car, as the driver pointed out a handful of famous sites on their long way around to the MacDonalds' house.

The MacDonalds welcomed them, warmly embracing Alex, and then turning to Lexie and Heather, and after only a moment's hesitation, embracing them as well. 'I'm so very glad that you all could come,' Phyllida said.

Alex looked at Heather as if to say I told you that you were welcome—needed not just by me. Heather smiled and he knew she understood. He remembered the way the MacDonalds—Phyllida and Andrew—they insisted they be called—had seemed to communicate effortlessly, completing each other's sentences. He never wanted to take Heather for granted or to lose the precious connection they had. He gave her shoulders a quick, wordless hug.

'After you've settled into your rooms, we'll have a little luncheon on the lawn,' Phyllida said.

Heather and Alex had a large room with a dark wood four poster bed and a view over the back garden. Lexie's room, smaller, was connected to theirs by a doorway. 'This used to be the nursery, years ago,' Phyllida explained, 'and the other room,' she nodded to Lexie's, 'was where the nanny slept. Much more comfortable now than in those days, I think. If you need anything, please let me know.'

Lexie girned about the size of her room and being stuck next to them, but, again, it was more an exercise than heartfelt. Moreover, Heather assured Alex both she and Lexie welcomed the closeness of their rooms here in this unfamiliar house.

Giles Rayburn, William's professor from the school of

art where he had studied photography, had opened a gallery not far from the art school when he had retired from teaching. As gracious as the MacDonalds, but preoccupied and nervous about the gallery opening, he joined them for lunch. He said he had some questions that perhaps Alex could answer if his family might spare him for a few hours?

Upstairs Alex, Heather and Lexie relaxed after lunch and talked over their plans. Alex wanted to be sure that Heather and Lexie were all right on their own before going to the gallery with Giles. With a quick hug to them both, Alex joined Giles Rayburn for the trip to the gallery.

'I haven't given much thought about William or that part of my life since his funeral,' Alex said as he and Giles climbed into his car. Alex didn't tell anyone about the nightmares or how hard he had worked not to think about that part of his life.

Giles nodded. 'I do need your help, but I thought a look before the event might be helpful for you as well.'

They came in through the back door of an odd shaped building in a part of Glasgow Alex didn't know at all. That didn't surprise him. He'd spent more of his life outside Scotland, and much of his time in Scotland was in Caithness—a world apart from even Scotland's own cities let alone the places he'd spent his working life.

'Don't be put off by the chaos just now. I have elves who'll be working through the night,' Giles said cheerfully if a bit wearily.

Alex felt once again the regret that he knew so little about William's life. Giles must have been important to William, but Alex couldn't remember any stories William had told about him. Their life had been their own world, dealing with trying to make sense of wherever they were—for themselves, for others. It left little room for other conversations, and thinking about home could be a dangerous distraction.

Alex gasped at the sight of the disarray in what was to be the exhibition space. Debris meant danger and the hypervigilance that had kept him alive kicked in—he looked for potential threats, fighting back memories of things he couldn't quite forget.

'It isn't as bad as it looks, I promise you,' Giles's voice cut through Alex's near panic. 'I was hoping you'd give me some background for these smaller photos here.'

Alex stilled his breathing and moved toward the photos in Giles' hands. Alex recalled not only the dates and places but also the scents and sounds captured in the photo. He gave Giles the necessary information and kept the rest for himself and William, as if jealously guarding it.

'Have a wander while I input the information for these to be properly labelled, then I can get you back to your family.'

On a table at the back of the gallery sat an album like an old fashioned family photo album containing clippings of articles he and William had done together. Alex flipped through the bulging album pages. He and William might have had a laugh over it, maybe even taken some pride in it, but on his own all Alex could think was, 'William didn't need me.'

Phyllida explained to Heather and Lexie as they walked in their garden, 'William's father and I met when he became a director for an organisation I was doing some work for, the ones hosting the dinner tonight if you'd like to come along.'

'Lexie said she'd rather stay at home if that's OK,' Heather explained, marvelling at how shy her daughter had become in this new environment.

'Of course, that's fine, Lexie. Some of William's cousins may be arriving tonight so you might have companionship closer to your own age. I hope you can join me, Heather. As a librarian I thought you'd enjoy the chance to see the Signet Library all dressed up.'

Heather said, 'It'll be a pleasure.'

'It's a sit down dinner so a posh frock is required. Have you brought something?'

Heather laughed with a lightness she rarely felt meeting someone for the first time, 'Wild Highlanders don't have much need of big city clothes, but I do have one nice-enough dress.'

'The one you got married in, mum?' Lexie asked.

'Yes, and you'll see it again tomorrow, too.' Heather said.

'Oh, I forgot to congratulate you,' Phyllida said, hugging Heather. 'We can talk more in the car, but I need to get ready. Be downstairs at 6:30?'

Heather agreed, and Phyllida hurried off.

'You like her don't you, mum?' Lexie asked.

'I do, don't you?'

'Yes, but they're different.'

'Different on the outside, sweetie,' she said hugging her daughter close to her. 'but inside, where it counts, just like us. She feels like someone I can talk to.'

Lexie, hugging her mum, 'I'm glad you have someone else to talk to.'

Heather didn't ask who the someone was. Did she mean

Alex or her own petite self. Had Heather leaned too heavily on her daughter for companionship?

'What's this place you're going to?' Lexie asked.

'The Signet Library? I know it's in old town near St. Giles. Let's look it up on your computer. I'm sure they'll have a web site—then you can go along with us while staying at home in your jim jams.'

The look on Lexie's face reassured her mum that Lexie was still her adolescent self, but she obligingly looked up the website for the Signet Library and mother and daughter both marvelled at the splendour and the long history of the Writers of the Signet and the charities they supported.

'So "Writers of the Signet" doesn't mean writers like Dad—it means lawyers, right?'

'Yes. Tonight will be about one of the charities they support. I'd better get ready.' Despite reassuring Lexie, Heather was nervous about her dress, her hair, her conversation. She liked Phyllida, and the idea of a night on her own as a professional filled her with joy and anxiety equally mixed.

As Phyllida and Heather pulled out of the drive, Heather saw Alex coming back with Giles Rayburn in his car. One glance through the window was enough for her to see that something was wrong. In her own excitement about the trip, she had underestimated how Alex felt seeing William's photos and revisiting his grief and loss—not just for William but for the life he'd left behind. She sighed and leaned back in the soft leather seat.

'Are you all right?' Phyllida asked.

'Alex. This is bringing back to him some painful things.'

'It's meant to be healing,' Phyllida said almost apologetically.

'Oh yes of course, I wasn't…'

'No, no, I didn't take it as a criticism. I just meant that it will hurt for a while but, hopefully, be the beginning of the end, at least of the worst part of it.'

Heather took Phyllida's hand. Beneath that composure she must be hurting, too. 'I'm sorry. I've been so wrapped up in my own thoughts that I forgot how hard it must be for you and your husband.'

'I'm so very glad you're here,' Phyllida squeezed Heather's hand and then the composure, the public self was in place and they rode the rest of the way in silence.

The Signet Library was more magnificent than any web site could show. Phyllida left Heather to explore the upper library while she went about the business of the evening. Heather looked at columns and giant windows reflecting the lights from the table settings and candles. She was admiring a giant stained glass window when a waiter came to show Heather to her seat. There were several people already seated around her table, but Phyllida was not among them. She was on the dais.

Between courses Heather's table companion asked her 'What brings you to our dinner tonight?'

'I'm a guest of Phyllida, Mrs. MacDonald.'

'Oh, Phyllida was a student of mine years ago. Please don't ask how many,' he said, shaking his head and smiling.

Heather relaxed a little and continued, 'My husband'— the word rolled around with its unfamiliarity—'is—was friends with the MacDonalds' son, William.'

'Would that be Alex. Alex Sinclair?'

Heather nodded.

'Your husband is a splendid writer. And a very brave man.'

'Thank you.'

'Have you come then for the showing at the gallery?'

'Yes.'

'I'll see you there tomorrow then as well. All of the Mac-Donalds' friends are hoping this exhibition will help them come to grips. This past year has been terrible for them, especially Andrew. I suspect it may be hard for your husband as well.'

Heather nodded, studying the dark red wine in her glass. 'He's spoken very little to me about his life with William.'

'That's often the way with such things,' he said.

Conversation became impossible then as the last of the dishes were hastily cleared, and Phyllida rose to introduce the speakers. Heather enjoyed hearing about research into the effects of literacy for women in reducing family poverty. By the time the speaking and presentations were over, however, Heather was tired and her thoughts were turning back to Lexie and Alex. Her dinner companion extended his hand and then gave her a kiss on the cheek and said, 'It's late for an old man, but I hope to continue our conversation tomorrow. I'm so very glad you're here.'

Phyllida arrived, 'I hope the evening hasn't been too tiring for you.'

'Not at all. Thank you. The place, the food, the company was brilliant. Literacy is a subject that I care about and the connection between literacy and poverty gave me something new to think about.'

'Wonderful! now let's get out of here; these shoes are killing me,' she said.

Once back in the car, Phyllida said, 'William mentioned that you and Alex had been childhood friends.'

'We knew each other from nursery on, but we weren't friends until the day of the wine-dark sea picture,' Heather said smiling, remembering fondly the story she hadn't shared with anyone for many years.

Phyllida laughed. 'I have to hear more about that.'

'My father loved Homer. He used to read it to us. I didn't know that wasn't what other children had for a bedtime story,' Heather shrugged looking at Phyllida.

'I was a bit older when I took on Homer myself, but no harm in it earlier I should think, leaving out some of the grimmer bits.'

'That's what my father said when my mum suggested Enid Blyton or Amazons and Swallows instead. So when one day in school we were told to draw a picture of the sea, I drew a purple sea.'

'The teacher, I'm guessing, was not a reader of Homer.'

'If so, she didn't expect me to be. I was in trouble with the "young lady, what is this" harrumph and all in front of the class all eyes on me.'

'You must have been embarrassed.'

'Mortified. Then Alex walks up, takes one look and says, "I think the wine-dark sea would have more red in it".'

Phyllida laughed, then, looking down at her hands, 'No wonder William loved him. I don't think Alex knows how much he meant to William, and thus, to us.'

'Alex has always known more about other people than about himself,' she said thinking how lost she had felt without him for all those years.

They rode the rest of the way home in silence. As they stepped quietly over the threshold, Phyllida turned to Heather and said, 'I need a cup of herbal tea to calm down. Join me?'

Heather shook her head No and slipped off her own shoes. 'Thanks, I want to see Lexie and Alex safely tucked in,' and she crept, shoes in hand, up the stairs through the sleeping house.

Alex didn't stir as she opened the door. Heather moved quietly to the adjoining room to look in on Lexie. She was asleep with her computer still on. Heather noticed the last entry on Lexie's Facebook page, a photo of the Signet Library with the comment 'My mum went here tonight for some meeting—bigger than Thurso library lol.'

It had been a long time since she had done something to make Lexie proud of her. Heather had told herself that it was just teenagers and their mums, but it had been more than that she realised now. What was that line from Tam O Shanter about nursing her wroth to keep it warm? She shook her head at the thought of how things might have gone if Alex hadn't come back. She was as blind to herself as Alex was to himself. She drew the covers around Lexie, closed down the computer, and returned to her own room—their room. She watched Alex's slow breaths in and out; his face, in sleep, only slightly older than that of the gawky boy she had known a lifetime ago now. In that quiet space she realised he could be going away again. She didn't know what pull those years might still have for him. She picked up a pen and began writing the first poem she had written in sixteen years. It wouldn't be finished tonight, perhaps never. She wrote the 'literacy of love' and crossed it out and wrote 'the consolation of love.' She wrote until she was ready to sleep. She slipped under the covers and curled herself around Alex. He stirred slightly in his sleep and murmured something in a faraway voice. Heather put her arm lightly, protectively around him.

## REMEMBERING WILLIAM

'You look lovely, both of you,' Alex told Heather and Lexie, but clearly he was on edge. Heather helped him fasten the buckle of the kilt and straighten his shirt. 'You seem a bit…' she began.

The words tumbled out of Alex. 'I don't want you and Lexie to be disappointed. Yesterday the photos were all over the place—not sure what we'll see on the walls or even if there will be anything done. Some of it might upset Lexie.'

'What might upset me?' Lexie asked, coming back into the room with a hair grip that needed her mum's help.

'Violence. Some of it too violent for you, I think, maybe. I don't want you having bad dreams,' he said and smiled trying to make light of his concerns.

Both Heather and Lexie looked at him with a what-you-are-saying-does-not- match-what-you-are-thinking expression on their faces.

'There,' Heather said, finishing Lexie's hair grip with a flourish and pulling the three of them close together in front of the mirror, 'I think we all look pretty good.'

Lexie laughed, 'Oh Mum,' but was enjoying the dressing up more than she was likely to admit. Alex looked at them with such great joy that for the moment there was no room for his fears.

A quick knock on the door followed by Phyllida's voice, 'The car will be ready whenever you are. We'll just go on ahead with Giles now.'

The three of them walked down the grand staircase to the waiting car wrapped in their own thoughts. When they arrived, the gallery was already crowded. Waiters moved adroitly through the clusters of people with their trays poised at just the right height for easy access. Alex quickly picked a glass of champagne for himself and Heather. 'I'll find some juice for you, Lexie.'

Lexie began to protest, but one look from her mother stilled her.

Alex finished his champagne and picked up another on his way to find juice for Lexie. Several people that he didn't recognise nodded or smiled at him. He was becoming more uncomfortable. He felt a fraud and he was afraid that Heather and Lexie would see that. He saw that Lexie had received juice—he hoped it was juice—from a waiter's tray, so he stayed put trying to be inconspicuous in a corner of the room.

Giles Rayburn stood on a slightly raised platform to be heard over the crowd and clinked on a glass so that people milling about stopped and turned to listen.

'Thank you all for coming tonight to help celebrate the life of a creative young man. As you all know, we lost William last year, but despite his too short life he has left us a legacy that will live on. This retrospective of his photos attempts to capture the gift that defined William. We are honoured tonight to have William's parents, Andrew and Phyllida MacDonald here.' He raised his glass to them.

'We are honoured also to have the man who worked with William in some of his most creative ventures, Alexander Sinclair. We've included some of that work here. Alex reminded me yesterday that writers prefer to be behind the scenes, so we'll let Alex's writing speak for him tonight.'

'On the wall at the left, your left, that is, you'll see William's student work, including the portfolio he submitted for admission, 'Autochthonous,' in which he celebrates his heritage as part of the First Nations in Canada. From that first portfolio I knew we had a remarkable talent. On the other wall, are photographs and exhibits he created himself from his journalistic photography, thus combining in a way that few photographers could, both the reality of his reportage and an extended narrative through his interpretation. Now without any more introduction, please look, enjoy, celebrate the creativity that is William's lasting gift to us.' And he stepped down to light applause and murmurs of appreciation.

'What does "Autochthonous" mean, mum? And what are First Nations?'

'"First Nations" is the Canadian term for what some Scots call "Red Indians". I think First Nations is a better word, don't you?'

'Don't worry, mum. I'm not gonna say something stupid or ugly. You don't have to use your librarian voice on me.'

Heather laughed and hugged her, '*Autochthonous* means native to a place,' she explained.

'Why didn't he just say so?'

'Words have flavours beyond their basic meaning, so he probably picked it for the flavours it had for him.'

Lexie looked quizzically at her mother, but she and Heather turned their attention to the photos on the wall.

Heather thought the ones from his portfolio with notes explaining the techniques used and details of the paper it was on spoke of a young man trying to find his way, like a writer looking for his voice. She remembered her own time at that age and Alex.

'Where's dad?' Lexie asked.

'He's probably caught up talking with someone. You heard what Mr. Rayburn said.'

Below the line of the larger, artistic photographs were smaller photographs less contrived than the artful ones, but still demonstrating—'clarity of eye' or something almost like the second sight her mum's people had claimed to have. Even the apparently casual shots of children playing showed an uncanny knack for capturing more than an observation. A photo of three children in a canoe on a still lake with an early morning mist rising filled her with incredible sadness: for its beauty, for the fact that the person who created it was gone, all of those things and more for which she had no name. She gave Lexie another hug realising how precious the little time they had together. Lexie looked up and stiffened. 'I think I should find Dad now.'

'He'll be along as soon as he can, I'm sure.' Heather smiled both relieved and upset that her daughter could read emotions, hers at least. She had leaned too much on her daughter. She resolved to be a better mother, but Lexie was right. Heather would have felt better with Alex there.

In the centre of the gallery, directly facing the door, nearly filling the wall, was a portrait of a single figure standing full length casually leaning against a tall birch tree as if he were part of the copse of trees. The photo captured exactly a person so much a part of the land as to be one with it, the sepia tones of the print reinforcing this sense. Turning the stereotypical 'noble savage' image on its head, the figure facing into the camera offers the faint smile of an indulgent grandparent welcoming the viewers into his world. The photograph was that of William's much loved grandfather, the caption said. A knot of people had collected in front of this compelling photo: even in its stillness, the figure in the portrait had the power to hold people's attention.

'That's why he called it *autoch…*' Lexie stumbled over the word.

Heather nodded. Her daughter, their daughter, was, as Alex had said, a quick study. With his support and encouragement, Lexie had begun using her curiosity, her willingness to learn new things. Without his help what might Lexie have become?

Just as Heather and Lexie moved toward the right side of the gallery whose theme, announced in large letters high on the wall was 'Before and After', she noticed her dinner companion from the previous evening heading toward them. Heather smiled to see a familiar face.

'Mrs. Sinclair,' he nodded, handing her a champagne glass.

'And this must be…' he handed Lexie an orange juice.

'Lexie,' her mother said.

'Alexandra,' Lexie replied, 'thank you for the juice.'

'It's good to see you again. Please call me Heather. "Mrs. Sinclair"—I'm not used to such formality.'

'Callum Henderson, at your service. Are you enjoying the exhibition?' he included both Heather and Lexie. They nodded. 'May I join you for this next part of it?'

Again they nodded and then Callum leaned in to say to Heather only, 'Some of these photos may be unsettling.' Then addressing them both, 'This photo, "Before" is the only photo that includes William himself. You can see that he is obviously hurrying to join the others before the timer clicks the shutter,' Callum explained.

According to the caption, the photo was of a young boy named Ahmad, his father, an older brother, three uncles, all clustered around an ancient taxi cab. The women, Ahmad's sisters and mother, are posed, reluctantly it seems, behind the taxi cab nearly out of the frame. Only Alex and William are smiling wholeheartedly.

The next photo shows the burned out taxi. The charred remains of the car fill the frame: blackened chassis, tires melted, the roof twisted out of its intended geometry, fragments seeming to wave in the breeze.

'Jesus,' Heather muttered, 'how can a photograph make us care so much about a taxi cab?'

'Because William cared so much,' Lexie said, and then added, 'Where's Dad?'

Whether she meant in the photos or right now at her side was not clear, but Heather was grateful now for Callum's foresight for Lexie's sake as well as her own. She hadn't appreciated how the photos would affect both her and Lexie.

Deliberately placing himself between Lexie and the photograph he described what they would see, "After," he explained, is the same photo with those killed a year later removed. The photo contains the person-sized shapes where the father, an uncle and Ahmad's brother had been.' He stepped aside then with a mumbled apology as if the crowd of viewers had been the reason for his manoeuvre and carefully watched both Heather and Lexie take in the photo.

'It might have been Dad,' Lexie said.

'Oh, God,' said Heather, realising how close death had come for Alex.

Callum steered them both wordlessly toward the back door for fresh air. If he were surprised to find Alex there, he gave no indication of it, 'Phyllida asked me to keep an eye on them,' he said to Alex. Before he could disappear back inside, leaving the three of them alone in the cool evening air of a Glasgow alleyway, Alex said, 'Please give our apologies to our hosts. We'll catch a taxi back to the MacDonalds' and have an early night.'

'Do they have pizza in Glasgow, Dad?' Lexie asked.

'I think we can manage that.'

Heather slept little that night despite an intense weariness because both Lexie and Alex were restless. More than once she opened the door to Lexie's room and pulled the covers, which had been thrown to the floor with her tossing and turning back on Lexie and sat on the edge of her bed until she fell into an easy sleep. When she headed back to her own bed, she was surprised to see Alex sitting up, anxious, 'Is Lexie all right?'

'Yes, yes. Just a lot of excitement. New ideas. She's had a lot to deal with this past year. She'll be fine.'

'And you?' he asked.

'Me? Oh yes. A lot for me to take in, too. I hadn't appreciated how powerful the photos would be. And how little really I know about your life.'

'My *former* life,' Alex said.

'I think we ought to go back tomorrow and look through it all without champagne or other people around. For all our sakes.'

Alex looked—worried, uncertain, pleased—in the half light of a long summer late night his face was impossible to read.

They slept then. Over breakfast they said they'd like to go back. The MacDonalds were delighted. They, too, wanted some time to look over the photos and hear any stories Alex would like to share. Heather had not envisaged sharing Alex, but it would be unkind, unfair not to let the MacDonalds have their own much needed time. The gap, however, between understanding it and feeling altogether welcoming to it must have played briefly across her face. Phyllida sensed this. 'Heather, I appreciate your including us in your family time.'

Andrew looked at his wife curiously then added, 'Of course. Thank you all for...' and his sentence trailed out as he finished a cup of coffee.

'I'm the one indebted to you,' Heather picked up her

cue in the round of courtesy conversation, 'for making this whole thing possible and welcoming us into your home.'

'We'll have the car come round at, shall we say 10 am? I don't think Giles is an early riser,' Andrew said, comfortable again now that he was in control of logistics.

Alex was able to share more of the stories behind the photos. He told them all that Ahmad's family had lost their rug shop and that was when Ahmad's father became a taxi driver. The car was all that they had left. 'That carpet I sent you, Heather, that was made by Ahmad's family.' He walked and talked them all around the displayed photos as well as some of the many not included in the exhibit. Lexie spent her time no doubt listening at least to some of the stories but apparently absorbed in the album of published pieces: Alex's words and William's photos.

Heather hoped that the stories were helping Phyllida and Andrew come to grips with their loss, but she was uneasy. Andrew grew more restless rather than less as he heard each of the stories Alex offered. He demanded of Alex things that he couldn't know or speak about, Had William talked about Edinburgh? Or their fishing trips in Canada?

Heather looked at Phyllida with alarm. It was apparent that beneath her composure she was worried, too. Heather began to understand Callum's dinner conversation. Beneath the social graces something unresolved was lurking. She realised Phyllida must have anticipated something like this as Giles Rayburn breezed into the gallery, 'Oh, what devotees of art you are, to be up so early. I've made us some coffee and brought in some croissants. Such hungry work.'

Heather smiled gratefully both at Phyllida's foresight—

and the grace of Giles Rayburn playing the wise fool. She gave him a hug, 'I just love croissants,' she said.

'Oh, one has to administer some culture to the wild ones from the North,' he grinned, winked at Heather and then quickly moved to take cups to Andrew and Alex, still locked in conversation in front of the last photo with Ahmad. Where Andrew was asking Alex with almost desperate urgency, Why hadn't William said anything to them about Ahmad? Had Alex kept in touch with colleagues in Afghanistan? With Ahmad?

'I don't know. No, that is not possible now,' they heard Alex saying.

'You have good friends, Phyllida,' Heather said.

'I hope I can count you among them, Heather, and that together we can…' she said looking anxiously at Andrew and Alex.

'I have faith in you and your friends. And I'm honoured to be included,' Heather said. She felt a comrade in arms with Phyllida, both of them involved in an undefined mission to help their husbands come to grips with loss.

Alex was able to join them, thanks to Giles's intervention. Too much talking, too much remembering, or something more imposed a weariness over the relief Alex had felt at first. Heather could see him struggling but could only hope that she would know how to help Alex when nightmares appeared again as she knew they would.

'If you ever come North, and I hope you will,' Heather said to Phyllida, 'there is a statue in Halkirk I'd love to share with you. Maybe not great art, but a brilliant metaphor. The only war memorial I know that is of a mother and child.'

'Please send me a photo of it, with you and Lexie in it, too, if possible. I haven't been further north than Perthshire for years. We,' she turned to look at Andrew, still apart from them staring at photos, 'plan to retire there. My parents' old house. It's been rented out now while we waited.'

Heather didn't need to ask 'waiting for what.' She understood all too well waiting for someone whose vocation competed with his love. She hoped she wouldn't have to face it again. 'If you wouldn't mind a houseguest, I might take advantage of some professional development available at the National Library. Your talk the other night reminded me how much I care about literacy and the impact it has on families.'

'Me, too,' Lexie added.

Both women looked at her, surprised. Lexie had seemed absorbed in her mobile phone.

'I mean, if that would be all right. Not the literacy part, or maybe. Would that be like being a tutor like dad? I think I'd like to do that.'

'You're always welcome, the both of you,' Phyllida said.

Heather suggested they needed to get ready to return. Andrew seemed still to want more stories, but Heather made some excuse about Lexie needing to be back. The unresolved grief from Andrew was palpable. It hurt to be near him, so Alex must feel that even more intensely.

Alex was silent as they packed, perhaps just tired. Lexie was more animated than Heather had seen her for some time. 'Did you mean that about wanting to tutor, Lex? I think you'd be good at it.'

'I guess so. I'd like to come back to Edinburgh and I

couldn't just sit around. William's cousins didn't show up. I think that made Phyllida sad or worried. I think it's like you said, mum. They're only different on the outside. I'm pretty sure she likes me.'

Heather marvelled at the wisdom packed into her tiny daughter. Not so tiny any longer. Lexie was on the brink of becoming the woman she would be, and Heather was privileged to be seeing it, to be a part of it. Jesus, she thought, when was the last time she had stopped to think what a gift it was to be a mother, not just a mother, but Lexie's mother. She stood with her dress—one and only good dress—poised above her suitcase lost in the wonder of it. Lexie came back in, her suitcase packed, 'Do you need a hand, mum?'

Phyllida went with them to the train, but Andrew, still preoccupied, said goodbye at the house. Alex slept for the first part of the journey. Heather and Lexie talked and dozed and watched the panorama out the window. When Alex woke, he looked crumpled but refreshed. Any ghost-memories seemed to have been left behind.

They changed trains at Perth. 'Is this where Phyllida and Andrew have their retirement house?' Lexie asked.

'Somewhere in Perthshire,' Heather said.

'I don't get the sense Andrew is ready to retire any time soon, do you?' Alex asked.

'No, not Andrew. But Phyllida is.'

'Andrew seems stuck with his bad memories. The photos were meant to be an end, but it re-ignited an idea he can't let go of that he needs to find Ahmad,' Alex said.

'Ahmad? The boy in the photos. Why?'

'William was fond of Ahmad. We all were, but especially

William, and now Andrew thinks the answer to all his pain is finding Ahmad. I should never have mentioned him to William's father. I should have kept it to myself.'

The train arrived and as they left the station the concern faded. Alex and Lexie invented silly games and then argued about the rules. Heather fell asleep listening to them counting, no doubt exaggerating, how many deer they saw as the train rolled through the golden brown hills toward home.

# THE BLACK BAG

Edinburgh and the exhibition had been a watershed for them all, but none of them spoke about it directly. 'I think I'll submit a short essay for that collection, *Afghanistan, War and the Media: Deadlines and Frontlines.*' Alex said.

'The title sounds a bit…' Heather waved her hands abstractedly.

'Academics are putting it together. It grew out of a conference in which those on the ground and those in the ivory tower trying to find common ground, a way to explain how things got so confused. I've read the essays submitted so far. They're uneven, as you'd expect in a collection, but good in many ways.'

Heather didn't ask what he meant by 'good'. She was content that Alex had a goal and was able to write about Afghanistan. He had often said he wouldn't write a book about it. Perhaps this was a safe compromise.

Lexie, too, had decided to become a literacy tutor. She ran her sessions in the library. Heather, trying to stay out of her way and yet keen to see her, occasionally caught a glimpse of Lexie from behind a fringe of a bookshelf. Lexie seemed absorbed and at home with her work helping younger students with basic reading skills.

Heather signed up for professional development, workshops on ways of implementing literacy programs and promoting them through social media. She wasn't optimistic of her chances, given budget cuts. Perhaps more importantly she had her notebook of almost poems. She had forgotten both how much pleasure it gave her to write and how hard it was to get from that first thought-feeling to a finished poem.

They'd been back home for nearly four months when Lexie came home from school and nearly tripped over a large cardboard box in the foyer, 'What's the big box doing here, dad?' she called up the stairs.

'What box?' Alex asked.

Lexie heard the sound of his keyboard. When he was writing, he could ignore anything. 'It's from the MacDonalds.'

'Must be something for all of us then, go ahead and open it. I'll be down as soon as I email this essay.'

Lexie peeled back the sticky tape over the centre seam and pulled the top of the cardboard box open. 'It's a bag,' she said, 'a black bag. Like a footballer's bag or something.'

Alex was beside her then staring at the black bag and shaking his head, 'No. It's a mistake. It's not for me.'

Baffled, Lexie said 'But it's addressed to you. Here's a note from Andrew stuck inside this catalog. *A few things I thought you'd need to find Ahmad.*'

'Put it back, Lexie, please. Oh, God, your mother will be home soon. She mustn't see it. Help me get it to the garage.'

'What does he mean "to find Ahmad"?'

'Now I know why Andrew hasn't retired, but this is a mistake for all of us.'

'How a mistake, dad? What's wrong? Please tell me what's going on. I won't tell mum just tell me what's going on.'

'Can you come walking with me on the beach? I need to walk fast to get myself settled and then we'll talk, I promise. OK?'

They walked hard for nearly an hour. Lexie nearly running to keep up with Alex's frantic strides before he slowed and began talking, 'You remember those photos of William's?'

'Which ones?'

'Before and after.'

'Oh those.'

'The young boy in the photo, Ahmad, was very fond of William. William talked about making a home for Ahmad.'

'But he already has a home, doesn't he?'

'Yes, well, maybe. They lost their rug shop and then the taxi. I don't know if he has a home or not or where he is now.'

'What does this have to do with that black bag and with you?'

'That black bag is given to every soldier going to Afghanistan, Afghan, as they call it. The catalog shows the variations in equipment for mountain and other such deployments.'

'You're not a soldier, are you? I thought you were a journalist. Is that why the black bag is a mistake?'

'Journalists going to Afghanistan now have to be

embedded: that means, go along with the soldiers, and so they wear the kit—at least the essential bits of it like body armour and helmets.' As soon as he said it, he realised how unsettling it would sound to Lexie.

'Mr. MacDonald wants you to go to Afghan? To some place so dangerous you have to be with soldiers and wear body armour? I thought he was our friend.'

'He is, Lexie. It's just that he is desperate to get some part of William back and he thinks my going to Afghanistan can achieve that.'

'Do you even know if Ahmad wants you to find him?'

'No, Lexie, we don't.'

'We'd better get back. Mum will be wondering.'

'There you are,' Heather said as they came in. 'I've put a quiche in the oven. I wasn't sure when you'd show up. It'll be ready in a few minutes.'

'Do I have time to make a phone call?' Alex asked, giving Heather a quick hug.

'Yes, should be about 20 minutes. Lexie, could you help me make a salad and set the table?'

Lexie moved wordlessly to help in the kitchen. At first Heather thought she resented being asked, but then realised something more was bothering her.

'Are you OK, Lex, you're awful quiet.'

'I'm just thinking. I've put some wine glasses out for you and dad. That's good with quiche, isn't it?' and she was away before Heather could ask anything more.

Alex rang the MacDonalds' home phone while Heather was busy in the kitchen. Phyllida answered. After the pleasantries, Alex said he was calling about the black bag. He realised with a start that Phyllida knew nothing about it. She and Andrew completed each other's sentences for heaven's sake. How could she not know about it? Then he remembered his first conversation with Andrew after William's burial—*don't tell Phyllida anything yet.* Just when had he planned to tell her? 'Sorry to have bothered you. I'll ring back another time. Heather has dinner ready.' Even over the phone he could hear how hollow Phyllida sounded as she asked Alex to pass her best on to Heather and Lexie. He rang off. More worried than he had been.

He paused outside the kitchen, enjoying the aroma of dinner and ordering his thoughts. How was he going to explain the black bag to Heather? He sighed and stepped into the kitchen, 'Wine? What are we celebrating?'

'Lexie's idea.'

'I think here at home with food a little wine is OK if you'd like to try it, Lexie,' Alex said.

'No thanks. I have a lot of homework.'

'Did you get your article done for that collection of essays?' Heather asked Alex.

'Yes. I was finishing just as Lexie got home.'

Lexie rose from dinner, clearing her plate, and scampered up the stairs.

'What's with her?' Heather asked.

'She's doing her best to make sure I tell you something that she's afraid you don't want to hear.'

'What's wrong?'

'Nothing.'

'Then why the wine, the silence, the disappearing act?'

'It's about a black bag that arrived today from Andrew.'

'A black bag?' Heather shrugged.

So Alex told her about journalists and embedding and Afghanistan.

'Afghanistan?' Heather asked, her fear of losing Alex again rising against her best efforts to contain it along with anger at the intrusion into their life of Andrew's unresolved grief.

'I'm not going, Heather,' Alex said, rising and taking her hands in his. 'Andrew has it in his head that Ahmad will be the answer to his—emptiness—and that I must find Ahmad for him, but that's not the right thing for any of us. I'm certain of that now.'

Heather poured them both another glass of wine and waited for the words that Alex had been struggling to find for months now, his own way to come to grips with his grief over William, which he had kept so tightly bound within him.

Alex had finished his wine and begun to cry before the words came slowly out. 'I was the page 37 guy—you remember, the play it safe guy. William was brilliant. Possessed when he was after a shot. I was meant to keep him safe.'

'There's nothing you could have done…' Heather interceded.

Alex smiled up at her and ran his hand lightly over hers. He nodded, 'I know that now. It doesn't make it hurt any less, but the nightmares…'

Heather nodded. The nightmares had been something that she felt were all the words Alex could not find during the day making their way to the edge of his consciousness. In time, she had thought, he would share what he could.

'But William's father. At the exhibition. He is so like William was. It frightened me. I couldn't save William but somehow I have to save his father. I don't know what the answer is or even what I can offer to fill his emptiness, but I know the answer is not in Afghanistan.'

\*\*\*

Long after Alex had rung off, Phyllida had continued to hold the phone to her ear, as if there were no place to put this new information in their well-ordered home. She felt betrayed. Hurt, anger and the jealousy only a stepmother can feel left her reeling. Andrew was unable to share his son with her even in death. This black bag that Andrew had sent to Alex had opened a rift in their usually seamless life together. There had to be an explanation. She'd speak with Andrew.

'Alex called earlier about the black bag you sent,' Phyllida said over dinner.

'I'll ring back after dinner,' Andrew said. Only Phyllida's familiarity allowed her to notice a faint tightening of his lips.

'I don't recall your telling me about it,' Phyllida continued.

'No? Must've slipped my mind.'

'Perhaps now you'd care to share your thinking with me?' Even having to ask to be in his thoughts made Phyllida feel small, and that smallness made her feel angry. No doubt Andrew heard it in her voice. She made no effort to conceal it.

'Journalists now, for their own safety, have to be embedded and the kit can be expensive so I…'

'Don't you dare patronise me with your how to avoid answering the real question public persona, Andrew MacDonald. What I'm asking is what the hell do you think you're doing? Alex is William's best friend. Would you sacrifice him and his family for this obsession of yours?'

'Now you see why I didn't tell you, my dear.'

'Because I would tell you how wrong you are, Andrew, is that what you're trying to say?'

'I've never seen you like this.'

'You've never shut me out before. I don't like it. I like it even less that you've done it to play havoc with friends of ours—faithful, kindly people. Loyal to you and William and now you're betraying that loyalty.'

'Surely if they're loyal they'll want as much as I do to find Ahmad: to make things right.'

'You forget I'm an attorney as well as your wife. I know the rhetoric of evasiveness. Finding Ahmad, who may not want to be found, is not the same as making things right for you or me or William.'

'William is, was, the last of my line of MacDonalds,' Andrew said.

'Each of us is the last of something, Andrew. Another hole won't fix the first. William wasn't even my son and I know he wouldn't want Alex going back. Why can't you see that?'

Phyllida knew she had won the argument as surely as if she were reading a jury, but Andrew's obsession appeared untouched. With her anger dissipated, numbingly cold emptiness was growing inside her. She had never argued with Andrew, never really disagreed with him on substantive things. Neither of them knew how to manage this rift. 'I'll look in on the house in Perthshire. I'm missing trees,' Phyllida said standing up from the table.

Andrew, looking at the napkin in his hand, nodded, 'We'll retire there, won't we Phyll?'

Phyllida couldn't give him the reassurance he needed. His obsession consumed everything, leaving no room for her, for them. His grief had been all consuming for almost two years now. She was drained. She would not lie to him. The best she could manage was a silence. Her husband needed to find his own way to dispel the idea that Ahmad was the answer to his emptiness.

Andrew heard the front door close and Phyllida's car leave. He poured himself another whisky. He lost track of time and whiskies. It was nearly 2am when he rang Alex back.

The phone jangled Alex awake. He got to the phone quickly, hoping that the others might not be awakened, and took the phone into the corridor.

'Just returning your call, Alex. Andrew MacDonald here.'

Any relief at hearing a familiar voice was quickly drowned by the thick, awkward drunkenness of it. Alex thought of that Biblical story, who was it that covered up his father's nakedness? This was an Andrew he didn't want to see so naked, so vulnerable. 'It's late. My family's asleep. I'll call you in the morning.'

'Phyllida,' Andrew said.

'I'm sorry. I said something earlier perhaps I shouldn't have.'

'She would've found out some time about our plan.'

'I thought you and Phyllida talked about everything,' Alex said, hoping for some explanation.

'We do—we did—she's gone to Perthshire.'

'Perthshire?'

'Said she needed to talk to trees.'

'It's late. Heather and Lexie are sleeping. I'll call you in the morning.'

'In the morning,' Andrew repeated the way drunks do. Maybe understanding the words or hoping to avoid an empty house Alex thought as he put down the phone. Without Phyllida, Andrew must be desperately alone. He shivered in the cold and hurried back to bed. Heather was not sleeping but she lay still so he lay quietly next to her until sleep caught up with him. A sleep burdened with a dream in which he struggled with looming trees of kelp; whichever way he turned, the kelp clung to him. The more he struggled, the more entangled he became. And through it all he kept asking why would Phyllida want to talk to trees? He looked for her among the trees. He was alone. He woke to find the covers twined about his legs. He blinked to shake away the nightmare and listened for the reassurance of breakfast noises. Up the stairs along with the aroma of coffee and toast came Lexie's words, 'I'm doing a combined advanced higher in geography and English with Mr. MacLeod.'

'Mr. MacLeod? I thought you didn't like him…' Heather was saying as Alex walked into the kitchen.

'No one's ever done a combined geography and English project so only Mr. MacLeod was willing to take it on,' Lexie explained.

'So why a combined geography-English project?' Alex asked.

'Afghanistan,' Lexie said as if that explained everything. 'If some books come for me, go ahead and open them up, OK? Better than a black bag in the post,' she said, heading out the door.

'Thank God for Ian MacLeod,' Alex said, 'He looked after us and now he's there for Lexie. She has big ideas and a reluctance to do things the easy way.'

'I suspect our parents said the same about us,' Heather said, pouring them each a cup of coffee, 'Now about that phone call and whatever was chasing you in the night.'

Before he'd gone beyond assuring Heather that he would not go back to Afghanistan, the phone rang. Heather answered. Phyllida's excited voice began without preliminaries, 'We've been looking in the wrong place! What if Ahmad by the grace of whatever God you care to credit has already made it *here*? If I hadn't been blinded by... The point is we can do something right here right now for Ahmad or others so achingly like him. The way through grief has to be doing something. Andrew has been looking at the wrong something.'

Alex watched as Heather nodded at whatever conversation was on the other end of the call. 'I think I follow you, Phyllida,' Heather said looking at Alex. 'Hold on, let me put this on speaker phone so Alex can hear, too.'

'Hello, Alex, glad to speak with you. I was explaining to Heather that I think our best approach to help Ahmad is to start right here at home. I recently learned that the government is preparing to send back unaccompanied

Afghan children who arrived here seeking asylum just because they've turned 18. Apparently, young Afghan children—as young as 5 years old—somehow managed to make their way here unaccompanied and claiming asylum. They were put in foster care and then just because they turn 18, that care ends. They have to apply all over again for asylum, and very very few of them are getting it, and then they just get sent back to a country they know nothing about. I don't think we can let that happen, whether our particular Ahmad is among them or not, at least not without ensuring they really have the support that the government proposes for "reintegration centres" in Kabul. I need to meet with some friends and immigration lawyers, but I would hope that you all, Lexie, too, might join us down here to talk about an overall strategy. I think together we can make a home for Ahmad whether here or in Kabul. Sorry to be so rushed, but I need to get back to Edinburgh for those meetings.'

Heather put down the phone and she and Alex looked at each other. 'Must've been a helluva conversation with the trees,' Alex said. Heather nodded and Googled 'child Afghan asylum seekers'.

She and Alex streamed a BBC report that interviewed the young men and the foster families fighting to stay in the country they had adopted. There was no doubt that Phyllida had found a cause they could all get behind. Heather arranged some time off. As soon as Lexie came home from school, they bundled her into the car, along with her newly arrived books and the laptop so she, too, could see the BBC report.

'So,' said Lexie, climbing in next to the black bag on the back seat of the car, 'we're going to the MacDonalds'.'

'Yes. Phyllida phoned. She has an idea,' Heather said.

'That doesn't involve the black bag, right?' Lexie asked.

'Right,' Alex assured her.

'What does Andrew think of that?' Lexie asked.

Heather and Alex looked at each other and decided to answer candidly. 'We don't know.'

'So we're going to his house to tell him he's made a mistake.'

'Sort of,' Alex said.

'How?' Lexie asked.

'We're not sure right now, but…' Alex said, looking at Heather.

'It's a long ride. The two of you'll think of something,' Lexie said, and perched her books on top of the black bag, 'makes a good travel desk.'

'What are you reading, Lexie?' Heather asked.

'A poetry book for my project: *poetry is revered in Afghan culture*, did you ever hear any, dad?'

'I once saw an army lorry collecting Afghans and providing a defensive perimeter so that they could have a poetry session. I haven't heard of anything like that since the troops started being withdrawn.'

Lexie laughed to herself, 'What if instead of a war they had a big poetry slam?'

Alex smiled at his daughter. A little over a year ago she had balked at the whole idea of poetry, now she had taken it on with her own ideas.

'Why are you smiling, Dad, it's a good idea.'

'I agree. I was just thinking back to the day we read "Below Green Corrie". Remember that?'

'Yeah. You felt all kinds of funny talking about poetry. Mum told me you never liked poetry.'

'I said no such thing, Lexie,' Heather said.

'What *did* you say then?'

'I said he never understood *my* poetry. That's different.'

'Mm hmm,' Lexie said, 'so now do you understand Mum's poetry?'

'I haven't read any for years, Lex.'

'Don't you show him the ones in your notebook, mum?'

Heather blushed and shifted in her seat.

'I didn't know you were writing again, Heather, that's great,' Alex said. 'I've swotted up on poetry,' he grinned back at Lexie, 'so you might give me another chance.'

'They're not ready yet; I'm working on them. Maybe they'll be OK, maybe not. I don't know.'

They stopped for fish and chips at a well-known chippie as if it were a celebration, but both Heather and Alex felt increasingly apprehensive as they got closer to the Mac-Donalds' home. Lexie, engrossed in her project, looked up from one of her books and asked, 'Dad, what's a *subaltern*?'

'A junior officer in the British army. I don't think the term is used anymore. Why?'

'I'm reading about the first time we went into Afghanistan back in 18 something or other. Listen to this,' she said, reading aloud: '*Even a subaltern had half a dozen servants who looked after his glass, crockery, and portable bath tub.* Far cry from a black bag, eh, Dad? *260 camels* to a regiment. That must have been a sight.'

'Camp Bastion has a Pizza Hut and Kentucky Fried Chicken. Lots and lots of lorries, but no camels.'

By the time they arrived, the MacDonalds' house was dark except for porch lights and the soft glow from one window. 'Phyllida said Andrew would wait up for us,' Heather said. 'It looks as if he's in his study.'

Alex could read Heather's mood, anxious like his own, but Lexie had gone quiet, perhaps just tired. He took their bags out of the boot and then noticed Lexie tugging at the black bag, which seemed nearly as big as she was in the half darkness. 'This has got to go back to Mr. MacDonald. It's a mistake. His mistake,' Lexie was saying.

Something in her voice put Alex on edge. 'Here, Lex. Here's your bag. It's more your size. I'll get that one tomorrow.'

'No. No. It's got to go back. Got to go back *now*,' she said, her voice tight with fear, and tears rolling down her cheeks.

Seeing his independent, intellectualizing girl-woman transformed into tears stunned him. He dropped his bag and cradled Lexie in his arms as she sobbed, 'I won't let him take you away.'

'No no. No one will take me away, Lex.'

Heather took the two steps to reach them from the other side of the car, realising without jealousy that Alex might leave her, but he could never leave Lexie. She stroked Lexie's hair and said to Alex, 'Better bring that bag in, too, since it worries her so.'

They turned to see Andrew standing in the doorway. 'Heard your car come in,' he said by way of welcome in speech heavily laden with whisky.

Alex looked to Heather, putting her hands protectively around Lexie. 'If you can manage Lexie and your bags, I'll look after Andrew,' he said. Then to Lexie, 'Things are all'—he waved his hand—'confused right now, but it'll be OK in the morning. Go with your mum, OK?'

Lexie looked up at her mum and smiled weakly. 'Don't let him go away again, mum.'

'Your father will never leave you, Lex. We need to do what we can to help. For now that means getting out of the way, OK?'

Andrew stepped aside as they came in, 'Must be tired. Long trip. Welcome. Phyllida said…' and he looked around as if to find Phyllida at his elbow and then blinked up at Alex as if surprised to see him and began again, 'Must be tired…'

Alex had seen a three-day drunk before: stubbled chin, stale clothes, the slurring, the repetition of words, trying to forget the unforgettable and in the process losing everything else. He and William had put several journalists and a few soldiers to bed. Knowing the maudlin sentimentality might morph into dangerous aggression, Alex moved slowly and quietly. He took the glass out of Andrew's hand and moved in to support him at the same time propelling him forward and talking. 'Phyllida said you'd be waiting for us. Thanks for waiting up. One step there, easy does it.' By the time they'd lumbered halfway up the stairs, Alex was relieved to see Phyllida in her dressing gown heading toward them, looking worried and smaller in her dressing gown and loose hair, but still in charge.

'Phyll! Pleasant surprise to see you,' Andrew said, and then, 'Shhhh,' he put his finger to his lips and nearly toppled backward.

Together Alex and Phyllida got Andrew to the door of their room. Phyllida assured Alex she could manage from there.

Alex opened the door to their own room quietly and was surprised to see all the lights on and both Heather and Lexie huddled in the four poster bed looking at him intently.

He tried to smile away their concerns, 'Phyllida has him. He's in their room. I think he'll sleep. He'll have a helluva hangover to contend with.' He knew that tomorrow might be worse and so did they.

'I never saw anyone drunk like that. It made me dizzy to see it,' Lexie said.

'Dizzy?'

'Like when you look at one of those pictures that's meant to look one way and then somebody says "do you see the old lady" and you blink and try to see it that way… '

'An optical illusion?' Heather asked.

'Yes.'

'That's a good analogy, Lex,' Alex said, hoping he'd found his teacher-dad voice with his own head dizzy, full of too many things. 'It's late. How about some sleep?'

'I don't think I can,' Lexie said clinging more closely to her mum, her eyes still feverishly bright and red from crying.

'A bedtime story is what you need,' Alex said looking at Heather as if she would pull one like a rabbit out of a hat for them.

'Perhaps in the other room? Something left over from earlier times?' Heather said.

'I don't see anything here, Lex, but I'll read you what my father used to read to me.' He pulled out his much-mended ebook reader and called up the *Odyssey*. 'I'll just read tonight. I'll explain it tomorrow if you want to know more, OK?'

Already drowsy, Lexie snuggled into the covers and waited.

Alex went to a favourite passage and began, '*Ulysses, sole of all the victor train, an exile from his dear paternal coast, deplored the absent queen and empire lost…*' Lexie was soon asleep.

Heather, half dozing, propped herself on her elbow as Alex came back.

'Homer.' He said, holding up his ebook reader, 'It worked for us, so…'

'Not the horsehair crests and the battle for bodies?'

'No, no. Odysseus coming home. And for us, *And grey-eyed Athene sent them a favourable gale, a fresh West Wind, singing over the wine-dark sea*. Lexie's a wonder, *an empire nearly lost*. It wasn't the territory and all that stuff that was the treasure, was it, Heather, my absent queen?' he said and kissed her. 'Every time I read those lines I see more and understand how wise Homer was.'

After a short night's sleep, Alex lay in bed listening to the sounds of the house waking up. Heather had said she'd walk in the garden while he had a lie in, and Lexie, Alex thought, must still be asleep. He showered and dressed and then knocked on her door. When there was no response, Alex thought Lexie must already have gone down to breakfast or walking in the garden with Heather.

Alex was relieved to find Heather and Phyllida at breakfast in the sun room. No one mentioned the previous evening's events. The bright light streaming through the windows lifted his anxieties. 'Where's Lexie?' Alex asked.

'With Andrew in his study…' Phyllida said.

Alex took a long, thoughtful sip of coffee, 'I'll just look in on them.'

Alex opened the door onto a previously well-ordered room of desk and bookshelves and sofa to find what looked like a church jumble sale. The black bag had been tipped open like a cornucopia to reveal its contents. T shirts and underwear—long and short, socks and hats, a lightweight sleeping bag, dun coloured combat boots, trousers and smocks in the colours of foreign dust, combat goggles, acoustic hearing protection, and combat body armour—vests, pelvic protection, ceramic pads labelled 'this part away from body', tropical sweat rag, and hydration system—complete with its own cleaning kit were spread across the floor.

Alex stared at the contents, his breath coming short and sharp as his anxiety and anger rose.

Andrew spoke first, 'I thought unpacking it would help Lexie understand.'

Alex fought the urge to ask 'Understand what? Your insatiable grief swallowing us all?' and race across the room and whisk his daughter away from all this. He looked at Lexie and realised she seemed more in control than he was.

'I wanted to see it, Dad. It was my idea.'

'But,' Andrew continued, 'as I looked at it with Lexie, I understood that there is no solution in this black bag. I was wrong. I'll join you in a while.'

Lexie and her father closed the study door. Andrew was alone with whatever he had left of his defence against the incomprehensible loss of William. If there were words to rebuild the defences, Alex didn't know where to find them. Breakfast was quiet. Phyllida excused herself to collect the information she needed to share with them all she said, and to check on Andrew, Alex thought.

Phyllida had shared her idea with Andrew, but he had not been as responsive as she had hoped. For her, for them, this idea was a lifeline, 'Will you be joining us, Andrew?' she asked, walking into his study where he sat motionless with the contents of his black bag all around him, the debris of a mistake.

'But we'd never find *Ahmad*, Phyll,' Andrew said. 'The one William cared about. The one who knew him.'

Phyllida was silent for a moment. Then she said, 'That's selfish.' She held up a warning hand before Andrew could reply. 'Your grief,' she began, then turned to the window to steady herself for the hard words she hoped would call her husband back from his obsession, 'is a selfishness that William would not admire in you. Even when he could not love you, he never stopped admiring you. Now you have to honour what William loved most. Did William take those pictures, those years of pictures, so that people could wallow in their feelings, in their personal sanctimony? Is that what he gave his life for, Andrew? Was that his hope?'

She left space for him to answer now, but he did not. 'I knew him. You think I didn't; he thought I didn't, but I did. He took those pictures hoping that it would make people make it better. His whole life, he hoped. He died still hoping. And right now you have in your own sitting room the best of what William left behind, his friends, people committed to his ideals.' Andrew remained immobile. Phyllida closed the study door and did her best to steady herself. She had done all that she could for Andrew. Now she and Alex and Heather and Lexie would do all that they could for William and the things he believed in.

Heather, Alex and Lexie were waiting for Phyllida in the sitting room. 'Andrew will be joining us,' she said, answering their unsaid question. 'We each have talents that complement and overlap, so I think as a core team we have a lot of talent to bring to bear on what I see as a grievous injustice. These children managed to get here from Afghanistan against incredible odds and now they get very little attention, in violation of all kinds of agreements and protocols, not to mention decency.'

Alex smiled thinking he wouldn't like to be the bureaucrat on the receiving end of Phyllida's campaign.

'And with very little press attention, the notion of sending them back even worse off than when they arrived has less opposition than such a misguided policy should,' Phyllida continued.

'Media attention is no guarantee of political pressure,' Alex said.

'Of course, Alex, that's why I think our team can be so effective. We won't rely on a single strategy.'

Andrew came quietly into the room.

Phyllida smiled at Andrew. She was relieved to see him. Until that moment, despite her comment, Alex realised she hadn't been certain that he would join them.

'While we make the public aware of the situation, we'll also be taking a look at who profits from these children—in this country or in the proposed site of the "reintegration centre" at Kabul.'

'You mean like selling them?' Lexie asked, shocked.

'Not exactly, Lex. Orphan trains, poorhouses, there is a long history of exploitation in which people make money running the institutions that warehouse people or using them as cheap labour. I'm hoping, Heather, as librarian you might put together an annotated bibliography for the policy wonks behind the MPs and editors.'

Heather nodded, 'We might do something even with unexpected places like the Museum of Childhood.'

'What about me?' Lexie asked. 'What can I do?'

'Online researcher and youth ambassador,' Phyllida said.

'What does that mean?' Lexie asked, looking anxiously at her mother and father in turn.

'The author of that poetry book you're reading, Phyllida said to Lexie, 'she has a web site and she mentions others, doesn't she? That's where you'll start. Education will help give the orphans choices and make them more valuable as people in their own right. It sounds crass, but that will be important to some people. Even at the miserable way they're kept now, they're seen as a drain on the queen's purse.'

'And an unfortunate reminder of an unsuccessful and costly war,' Andrew said.

Speaking softly, Phyllida continued, 'We need to accept that we might not save all of these children. We might not save one of them. If we think otherwise, then each one lost will be a failure, a crippling blow to us and to them. They need to have faith in our good intentions as much as we do.'

Phyllida had assignments, which she handed out to

each of them. Heather, Alex, and Lexie would be working behind the scenes and so could work from home. They'd be in touch over the phone and in email: they were a team. Andrew's role was somewhat vague and he seemed subdued in his commitment.

Andrew joined Phyllida at the door as Alex was loading their car for the trip home. 'There was one thing in that black bag that's right for you after all in your life up there in the frozen north,' Andrew said extending to Alex a pair of thermal long johns and thermal shirt, tied with a ribbon with a lopsided bow, suggesting Andrew had tied it himself. Alex smiled and thanked Andrew. For the first time, he heard an echo of William's humour in Andrew's words. Although Andrew looked pale and subdued, he put his arm around Phyllida and together they waved goodbye. Thanks to Phyllida they had something to connect them, something besides an empty spot where William had been.

'This ambassador thing is going to be more work than school ever was,' Lexie said from the back seat reading over her assignment from Phyllida. 'Are we going to find Ahmad, Dad? I mean William's Ahmad?'

'Maybe, Lex, but like Phyllida said, we have to focus on doing what we can. As many Ahmads as we can.'

'And girls, too?'

'Girls, too, Lex.'

# EPILOGUE

Project Re-Home managed to work steadily through several years and different administrations. Heather's research, ironically, provided sound bites for politicians on both sides of the debate. Controversies arose from time to time: too much emphasis on Afghans or too little; alleged favouritism toward Dari over Pashto; or making Afghans into little Englishmen, which inflamed temporarily the chronic English-Scottish tensions. Some orphans were sent back; others chose to go back and re-join extended family. Some were granted asylum, including a group that settled in the western part of Sutherland where they provided a welcome population boost.

Alex published his book, *William and Ahmad.* He actively promoted it with interviews and readings around the world. Once done with that, he set up a small publishing company specialising in the writing of and about the North of Scotland

and said he hoped never to move beyond the North of Scotland again.

Just before Andrew and Phyllida retired to their Perthshire home, Phyllida made a trip North. On her way to visit the Afghans in Sutherland, she stopped to visit the Halkirk statue of mother and child that had, she told Lexie and Heather over lunch, given her the idea that had led to Project Re-Home. She gave Heather one of her own paintings of the big trees that she loves, 'Not enough trees up here for me, but otherwise a lovely spot, this Caithness of yours.'

Heather networked the Highland libraries and connected writing groups and literacy groups. With the firm persuasion of her husband and daughter she published a volume of her own poetry.

Lexie's Afghan poetry and place project took high honours. She continued her interest and friendships with Afghan women writers and the youth branch of the literary society online. While both her mother and father were content to stay in Caithness, Lexie found herself, now a professor at the University of Edinburgh, an honoured guest at an International Symposium in Kabul on poetry, place, and gender.

Women, poets, and foreigners were a volatile mix even now in the comparatively stable times after the war, so heightened security was everywhere. Any visits outside the hotel were meant to be limited to the accompanied bus trips pre-arranged. Lexie, however, had slipped out once or twice, remembering her father's words that it was sometimes easier to get in and out anonymous and alone. She needed to feel the very bones of this country. Both her parents would understand that.

Project Re-Home had done much good. They'd never found William's Ahmad. Although they all felt that gap, none of them spoke of it. Lexie had arranged for a visit to the orphanage and school that had begun as a reintegration centre for some of the asylum seekers in Britain. She was relieved to see that it was not the Dickensian horror that she had imagined. All the school children were lined up for a formal inspection as if she were the queen, as she stepped out of the car. They looked scrubbed and shiny and stiff in their formal clothes, but every one was smiling. A genuine smile that comes from a safe home, a faith in a future. Lexie nearly cried with the joy of it.

She accepted a bouquet of flowers from one of the older girls. Lexie thought the girl was probably about the age she herself had been when she had first learned about asylum seekers and war ravaged Afghanistan.

The head teachers then dismissed the children. The younger ones scampered noisily away despite the instructions they had been given no doubt. The older ones lingered, perhaps out of curiosity.

Lexie was led then through the school: classrooms, library with books in English as well as Dari and Pashto. The librarian was pleased to show Lexie her father's books and her own.

There was a computer lab. Lexie was delighted to see the up to date computers. One of the last things Phyllida had done before retiring was to get a grant from IBM for computers and ongoing upgrades. Lexie was pleased to see it being used. She smiled at a handful of boys working at the computers.

'We are most proud of a unique contribution from one of our supporters here in Afghanistan. Let me show you first in this next room, then we'll come back here to the computers.'

Lexie was led into a room with several looms in it and girls were working at the looms tying the knots of the traditional rugs that are an important part of Afghan culture. 'Oh, I've never seen how it's done, may I have a look?' Lexie said moving toward a young girl whose hands flew so fast over the pieces of wool that the carpet seemed to grow as if by magic. To the girl she said, 'When I was a girl, my mother had a carpet like this and I thought it was a magic carpet on which I could fly.'

The translator explained her words, and the girl laughed, covering her face. 'No flying on this one, I think.'

'Now you've seen the rugs, let me show you what our supporter, a designer who lives up in the hills, has done for us here.'

The young man at the computer had anticipated Lexie's return and had called up a program that allowed designs to be selected from a library of designs and adapted for any size and printed out for the cartoon, the map, used to create the complex designs on the carpets.

'In this way, our students can learn the designs. Some of them we had thought were lost forever because there have been so many casualties. But we are not stuck in the past either. There is a designer tool that allows new designs to be created, either from old motifs or by interfacing with this program to create new shapes, and even it is possible to combine them.'

'What a marvellous gift. Who is this supporter? Can I meet him?'

'Alas, no. He is a man that lives apart from people now. The war. Some people now only feel safe in a limited way.'

'I understand,' Lexie said, 'Please pass along to him how wonderful I think his gift is.'

Lexie's guide seemed visibly relieved at her easy acceptance of the absent supporter. 'He knew of your coming and asked especially that this be left for you,' the teacher said, handing her a paper-wrapped bundle tied loosely with string. 'Now, forgive me, but it is late, and I need to see to the children. Your car is waiting.'

Back in her hotel room, Lexie opened the package to find a small carpet very like the one on her mother's sofa back in Caithness. She ran her hand over the smooth surface of the soft wool, a kaleidoscope of colours in a complex pattern and remembered how she had thought it was a magic flying carpet. With her finger she traced the graceful curving line of creamy white against the dark blue background. That pattern had always seemed like the foam on the waves of the ocean outside her window in Caithness. What does it mean to someone so far from the sea?

She pressed her fingers into the carpet surface and thought of all the knots it took to make even a small carpet. She had never seen even a photo of Ahmad's carpet store. She closed her eyes and tried to imagine all that she recalled from her father's stories propelled through time. She tried to imagine the young Ahmad as a father, a businessman with a store again filled with the carpets that spoke of tradition and continuity in the midst of so much brokenness. And his gift to the school. Her father had been right. Ahmad had not wanted to be found—then or now.

On the top of the hotel stationery the receptionist gave her, she wrote 'Thank you,' in English, Dari and Pashto, the only word she knew in all three languages and that only in transliteration.

And then in English, the only language she had for poetry, she wrote

> *Beneath the surface soft and smooth*
> *A thousand thousand knots that bind us*
> *close*
> *despite a sea between us.*

# FOR MORE INFORMATION

Some of the sources that helped shape this story include the following. Web sites are dynamic. Addresses were current at time of publication.

I first learned about the young Afghan asylum seekers who had arrived as unaccompanied children and been put into foster care from a program that aired on BBC News Program, by Chris Rogers, July 2015, but it seems that returning them to Afghanistan when they turned 18 had been going on for some time already at the time of the program's airing. http://www.bbc.com/news/magazine-33524193?

*The Afghan Connection.* George Pottinger. Scottish Academic Press Ltd; First Edition, Dec. 1983

*I am the Beggar of the World: Landays from Contemporary Afghanistan.* Translated and presented by Eliza Griswold. Photographs by Seamus Murphy. Kindle edition 2014. Farrar, Straus and Giroux

*Load Poems Like Guns: Women's Poetry from Herat, Afghanistan.* Translated by Farzana Marie. http://farzanamarie.com/farzanamarie/Books.html

Lost Voices of Afghanistan grew out of Jonathon Charles' request to hear Afghan poetry.

http://www.bbc.co.uk/worldservice/mobile/documentaries/2011/01/110119_doc_lost_voices_afghanistan.shtml

*Afghanistan, War and the Media: Deadlines and Frontlines.* Edited By Richard Lance Keeble, John Mair. Published 2010 by arima publishing. www.arimapublishing.com

Andrew Motion won the Ted Hughes award for poems created from interviews with returning soldiers, *Coming Home.* I heard it on BBC Radio 4 Sat 15 Nov 2014

19611297R00072

Printed in Great Britain
by Amazon